FAKE

———

BETH YARNALL

FAKE

ebook ISBN: 9781940811970

print ISBN: 9781940811581

For the survivors of domestic violence—the ones who got out —and for those still looking for a way out.

And as always, to my husband, Mr. Y, for buying into and supporting every single one of my crazy Lucy and Ethel schemes...including the one where I thought I could write a book.

1

L ucy Monroe stood outside the thick wooden door with the gleaming brass nameplate, preparing to beg someone she couldn't stand for something she didn't want. Tugging at her slightly too-tight blouse, she hoped she hadn't overdone the perfume in an attempt to mask the stale stench of desperation. And desperate she was or else she wouldn't be standing outside of Cal Seller's office door.

Tossing back her hair, she rubbed her lips together and took a deep breath. She raised her hand to knock, pulling the gesture at the last moment before she rapped on the chest of the man who suddenly opened it.

"Well, hello, Lucy." Cal set his hand on the door-frame, blocking her entrance with six feet of lanky, overconfident cowboy. If he was surprised to see her, he didn't show it. His gaze traveled over her leisurely, not stopping to admire anything in particular as though he'd seen the view a thousand times before. Her body reacted as if he'd stroked her, aroused despite her burning hatred for him.

When he'd looked his fill, he stepped back, motioning her into the room. "Come on in."

"Er, ah, thank you." Chin high, she strolled into the room like she had a right to be there and hadn't told him to shove the job she was here to get back where the sun don't shine. As though she hadn't rubbed her new marriage and pregnancy in his face with the giddy glee of a teenager who'd snagged the star quarterback and wanted her cheating ex-boyfriend to know it. *Oh, how the mighty have fallen*, she thought. And fallen hard.

"Have a seat." Cal waited for her to be seated before sliding into the high-backed, leather chair at his desk. Behind him the Dallas skyline gleamed in the heat of mid-day. He reclined back, regarding her with those same cool blue eyes that used to rake her over as if he could see through her clothes. "What can I do for you?"

He'd asked her that same question before under entirely different circumstances. Naked and panting circumstances. Teasing and pleasing circumstances. Right here on top of his desk, her legs hooked over his shoulders... She cleared her throat and those memories from her brain, struggling to keep in mind the real reason she'd come here today. Her daughter, Poppy.

"You're going to need a new host for *Pleasure at Home*. At least temporarily. I can help." There. That didn't sound desperate, it sounded helpful. She was doing him a favor really. And if that favor turned into a permanent job for her, then so much the better. Cal loved win-win situations. Especially if he was the one doing all the winning.

"You're looking for a job?"

She was looking for more than that. What she needed was a miracle, a way to hold on to what little she had left. "My daughter will be eight months old next week."

He inclined his head in acknowledgment. Of course he knew that, nothing passed Cal's notice.

"I thought it was a good time to venture out and explore my options." Which were exactly zero. Unless she counted working retail with its long hours and measly pay. And how would she protect Poppy if she was never home?

"So you ventured my direction."

"I figured with Mi going out on maternity leave in a few months I could fill in for her. It's not like I'd need to be trained. I cohosted the show with Mi for two years before...before I left."

"Yes. I remember."

This wasn't going well. She could tell by the way the right corner of his lips had tugged up along with his eyebrow as soon as she'd opened her mouth about resuming her old job. She used to call it his *oh really* look. That mocking, *I'm in the driver's seat* tilt of his lips and brow set off all the warning bells inside her. He was plotting something. Something dangerous for her.

She stupidly plowed ahead anyway, too needy to walk away from what might be her last chance. Her only chance. "Yes, well, I thought I could start right away. Mi and I could cohost like we used to until she leaves, and then I could host alone until she comes back." And hopefully she could parlay that temporary into permanent.

"What happened to your... How did you put it? Ah, yes. Your husband's aversion to his wife prostituting herself by selling sex toys on TV."

"That was an unfortunate choice of words on my part. I apologize."

"Unfortunate. Yes. But still a problem for you, unless something's changed?"

The bastard. He knew. And now he was tormenting her by trying to make her confess what an idiot she'd been, how her life had crashed and burned. She thought about her daughter, and all her prideful anger drained away, leaving her more desperate than before. She'd do anything to protect Poppy. Anything.

She picked at the skin beside her thumbnail, knowing she had to tell him in order to get him to give her back her old job. An extremely well-paying job. A job she needed more than her next breath. "I'm not married."

"I thought you didn't believe in divorce."

"I'm not divorced."

"An annulment?"

"No." Damn him. "It turned out my marriage wasn't legal."

"Not legal? It seemed perfectly legal from where I sat in the church."

She'd invited him out of spite. She imagined he had attended out of pride. Their relationship—so passionate and exciting—had ended in barbs and jabs meant to wound. Now that too was coming back to bite her in the ass. *Keep your cool. Don't let him see you sweat. He thrives on the weaknesses of others. Don't be weak.*

"I thought so too," she said, sounding more confident than she felt. "Unfortunately he was already married when he married me."

"I see."

"So there's no conflict. I can start right away, or whenever you need me."

"But I don't."

"Don't what?"

"Need you."

She bolted up out of her chair, toppling it backward. "You son of a bitch! You let me sit here and spill my guts to you, knowing all the time that you weren't going to hire me back?"

"Sit down."

The door behind her opened. A willowy brunette with the body Lucy used to have poked her head in the door. "Is everything all right in here, sir?" She cast Lucy a look like she'd be happy to have her escorted out.

"Everything's fine, honey," Cal answered.

Thank God this wasn't *the* Honey Cal had employed back when Lucy had worked for him, but she was made from the same mold. Cal called all of his assistants *Honey*, and they all looked like they'd been ordered from the *Playmate of the Month* catalog. Rumor was that Cal's *Honeys* did more than run reports...a lot more. Unfortunately Lucy knew all too well the rumors were based in fact.

Cal's *Honey* gave him a look that could melt ice in a

snowstorm. "You let me know if you need anything, sir. Anything at all."

"Thank you. I will." Cal waited for *Honey*—or Felicia McAdams as the nameplate on her desk read—to close the door before turning his attention back to Lucy. "Please, sit down."

She folded her arms across her chest. "Why? So you can humiliate me some more?"

"You need a job, and as it happens I might have one for you."

"But you just said you didn't."

"I said I don't need you to fill in for Mi. Her sister-in-law will start cohosting with her today and then take over while she's on leave."

"So what's the job then?"

"Sit down and I'll tell you."

Cal waited with the patience he used to close multi-million-dollar deals for Lucy to right her chair and sit her pretty little ass back down. Truth was he knew why she was here and what she was going to ask before he'd even opened the door to find her standing on the other side. His gut twisted, thinking how desperate she must be knocking at his door. It was his fault she was in the straits she was in. He'd kept tabs on her, but apparently not close enough.

She'd shown up sooner than he'd expected, but as it turned out she'd come at a time when he'd just gotten his ass handed to him and was feeling a bit beaten up. Funny that sparring with Lucy had him rebounding with the energy of a champ. She always brought out the best in him. And the worst.

Lucy sat at the edge of the chair and crossed her arms and legs. "Well?" she demanded.

Now this was going to take some finesse. He'd been chewing over this predicament for some time and then he'd opened the door to Lucy and the solution had very nearly tumbled right into his chest.

"It's a bit high profile," he began.

She squared her shoulders and lifted her chin. "I've been on TV. That's the tiniest bit high profile."

Damn, but he'd missed her spirit. And her smart-assed mouth, and the way she tossed her blonde hair when she expected to get her way. He'd missed a whole lot of things about her, including the way his body reacted to her.

"The hours are fairly flexible," he continued. "You have a reliable babysitter who can work days and evenings?"

"I do."

"Good. Good. And you don't mind dressing up?"

She narrowed her eyes at him. "What kind of *dressing up* are we talking about?"

Now she had him remembering the time she'd worn that pretty little cowgirl outfit and had ridden him bareback...backwards. It fit with what she thought of him, he supposed. Pervert, bastard...what else had she called him? Ah, yes. A lowlife, two-timing son of a bitch with a dick for brains.

Maybe she was right. He certainly hadn't been able to accurately access the head he *should* be using ever since she'd strolled into the room and stroked him with the scent of her perfume.

He leaned back in his chair, stacked his boots on his desk, and clasped his hands in his lap. The blue of her eyes was barely visible now. She'd narrowed them into slits that told him his window for possibly winning her over with his idea was quickly closing.

"Not that kind of dressing up." He'd keep this to business if it killed him. "Cocktail dresses, ball gowns that sort of thing."

She tilted forward in her chair a little and uncrossed her arms to stack them on her knee. He hadn't gotten to where he was now without being able to read an opponent's body language to know when things were starting to swing his direction.

"Would they be provided?" she asked. "Or would I have to come up with the money to rent them out of my salary?"

"They would be provided. You'd have an expense account for whatever you'd need."

"And what exactly would my duties be?" She was interested. Good.

"Charity events, dinner parties, corporate functions, hostessing, that sort of thing."

"Sounds more like something you'd need a wife for than a corporate employee."

"That's exactly what I need. A wife."

She put up a hand palm out. "Hold up. You're asking me to marry you?"

"Yes. For at least a year...maybe a little longer."

She exploded off her chair, propped her hands on her hips, and leaned over the desk at him. "What kind of dim-witted dumbass do you take me for?"

"No kind."

She turned and snatched up her purse. "I don't know what kind of joke this is supposed to be, but I'm not going to be any part of it."

She started for the door, but he was faster, getting there ahead of her to block her exit.

"Just hear me out."

"No. Hell no."

"You need a job. I need a wife. I'm in negotiations to buy a company that could turn Sellers Investments into a multinational corporation. But my board is packed with a bunch of traditionalists. They've been after me to clean up my reputation and won't agree to the purchase unless I make some significant changes."

"They don't want their company headed up by a man-whore? I'm shocked. I also don't see how paying a woman to marry you—especially one who can hardly stand the sight of you—is going to improve your reputation. And isn't that prostitution anyway?" She jabbed him in the chest with her sharp, pointy fingernail. "If you think I'm low enough that I'd prostitute myself to you, then you're an even bigger dickhead than I thought."

Well, shit. This all had sounded so much better in his head. "No. Never that, darlin'."

This was supposed to be a deal where he'd help her get back on her feet. The fact that it also helped him was a distant third. Ridin' second was the hope that maybe they would end up in bed together, but now she'd gone and made it all feel so unseemly.

"Really? Because paying a woman to sleep with you *is* prostitution. Look it up."

"I wouldn't be paying you to sleep with me. I'd be paying you to be my wife. The sleeping-with-me part would be optional."

She blinked slowly up at him. "Optional." At least she'd retracted that nail.

"I need a wife. You need a job. This is a sound business agreement."

"And what makes you think I'd want to sleep with you, optional or not?"

His gaze dropped to her mouth. He wanted to answer her with a kiss that would make her remember just how damn good they'd been together. How goddamned hot they'd been for each other. And maybe get her to look at him like she used to and not how she was looking at him now. He was damn sick and tired of being the asshole who'd broken her heart by being the careless, unthinking bastard he was.

"I'll give you a twenty percent raise over your original salary. You and your daughter would come live at my house—for appearances—all expenses paid."

"Oh, like a frat house bed-and-breakfast. Yes, that's exactly the environment I want my daughter raised in while her mother prostitutes herself for a twenty percent salary bump."

"Stop using that word. That's not what this is about and you know it."

"All I know is that you haven't changed one damn bit."

She tried to go around him, but he sidestepped and

she slammed into his chest. He gripped her by the arms to keep her from stumbling. Before he knew what he meant to do, he was kissing her the way he'd wanted to from the moment she'd appeared in his doorway.

His body recognized hers immediately, reacting instantly to the feel of her curves pressed up against him. She resisted at first and then it was as if her body recalled his as well, and she came at him like a bull out of a shoot, going from zero to all over him in thirty seconds or less. Goddamned if he burned hotter and brighter with her than with anyone else he'd ever been with.

He gripped her ass, bringing her fully against his growing erection. The lushness of her, the sounds she made, that thing she did with her tongue...fucking Christ. How had he gone a day without her, let alone nearly a year and a half? He turned them, pressing her between his body and the door.

They'd been in this position before. He'd taken her rough and fast, hardly thinking at all about what was on the other side of the door. He hadn't even taken the time to pull her panties down. He'd just shoved them aside and thrust deep, needing to be inside her more than he'd needed his next breath. That need was building now, threatening to break his infamous control.

He eased back and looked down at her. Her full lips were swollen from his kisses, her eyelids heavy with desire. Her breaths came in short pants that told him she was as turned on as he was.

"I *have* changed," he told her, whispering the words,

wanting her to feel his sincerity. "This between us hasn't. And it never will." He stepped away from her, trying to show her the change he'd just bragged about. "But it will *always* be optional."

She wiped the back of her hand over her mouth, considering him—he hoped in a new light. "You're the craziest son of a bitch I've ever met, you know that?"

"Maybe. Maybe I'm just a businessman who enjoys a well-negotiated business deal."

"Is that what you call bending your *honey* over your desk—negotiating a business deal?"

"No. That's what I call a mistake. Because that's what it was."

"Call it what you like, but I don't think you'll ever really change, no matter how many deals you *negotiate*." She fumbled for the knob behind her and opened the door.

He didn't stop her. He'd done all he could to convince her. "Consider my offer, darlin'." But he knew she wouldn't. He'd screwed everything up by kissing her. She didn't do well with pressure. Like an unbroken filly, you had to come at her from the side, sweet-talking and reassuring with a lump of sugar in your palm. But damn if the ride wasn't worth all the effort.

Lucy bolted out of Cal's office like her tail was on fire when it was her whole body that was ablaze. She wasn't sure which was making her hotter—anger or arousal. With Cal it was always so hard to separate the two.

She marched past Felicia's desk, down the long hall to reception, and out to the elevators. *Consider his offer.*

What she was considering was getting her daddy's Smith & Wesson and filling Cal's lying, cheating ass full of lead. Changed. Right.

She jabbed at the elevator button. The only thing that had changed was a new little trick with his teeth he'd learned from someone *somewhere* that had her grinding against him like a sex-starved bitch in heat. *He'd* picked up new tricks in the past seventeen months whereas the only thing she'd picked up was an extra fifteen pounds of post-baby weight that wouldn't come off.

Goddammit. She was actually tempted by his offer. She'd seriously considered it even as she'd accused him of trying to turn her into a whore. His whore. The truth was she needed the money. She needed a job with flexible hours so she could spend time with Poppy. But most of all she needed the security of living in Cal's house so she could protect her daughter.

But she wouldn't do it. She hadn't stooped so low that she'd sell herself to Cal Sellers like one of his prized heifers. No way in hell.

2

Lucy pulled up to her mother's house in Arlington, outside of Dallas. Spring was asserting itself early, scorching a path across North Texas that heated up the earth like a big ole electric blanket you couldn't turn off.

She was late picking up her daughter. She'd had to work an extra half hour to make up the time she'd taken to go all the way to downtown Dallas to Cal's office on what had turned out to be a fool's errand.

A car she didn't recognize sat in the driveway. Maybe one of her mother's friends was here for a visit. She angled out of the driver's seat and came up the drive instead of the walk so she could check out the car. Nothing on the seats or dash gave away anything other than it being a rental. She didn't like this one bit. A prickling at her nape had her quickening her steps. All she could think of was getting to Poppy and making sure her daughter was okay.

She opened the door—not bothering to knock—

and went right on in. Her mother came up off the couch, no doubt with a reprimand on the tip of her tongue, but Lucy didn't give her a chance to spew it.

"Where's Poppy?"

"That's not the way—"

"Where's my daughter?" Panic crawled all over her. "Where is Poppy?"

"Right here."

Lucy turned to see Kevin Walker, the no-good, rotten, polygamist bastard she'd thought she'd married, holding *her* daughter.

The last time she'd seen him he'd been standing over her, screaming obscenities, while she tried not to move or do anything to provoke him further. His anger was a near-tangible thing that whipped out and lashed at her, turning her handsome husband into an out-of-control monster who terrified her.

Kevin smiled as though he had every right in the world to be there. He didn't. She had a restraining order out on him for God's sake. He wasn't supposed to go within five hundred feet of her home or work, but it looked like he'd found a way around that—her mother.

"What are you doing here?" she demanded, trying to keep her voice even and not scream like she wanted to so she didn't scare Poppy. "You don't have visitation rights."

"Well." Her mother, Nadine, stepped forward. "I thought it would be good for Poppy to spend some time with her daddy. A girl needs her daddy."

A girl didn't need a lying, cheating, scary-assed

bastard of a daddy. Lucy would know. Her own daddy had been just like Kevin.

"What Poppy needs," Lucy said, walking over and prying her daughter away from Kevin, "is for Kevin to follow the rules the court set out. There's a reason he's not allowed to be around us, *Mother*."

Poppy started to fuss, putting her fist in her mouth. She must've sensed the tension in the air. Lucy held Poppy to her and nearly gagged when she smelled Kevin's after-shave on her baby.

"I have a right to see my child," Kevin had the nerve to declare. "Prepare to be served. I'm taking Poppy back to Utah to live with me."

What in the hell had she ever seen in him? He'd been charming and she'd been hurting and then before she knew it she was standing at the front of the church next to a man she hardly knew. She'd gotten a good taste of the real him a few short hours after they'd been married. He'd accused her of looking at Cal like she should've been looking at him, and he'd hit her. He knew how to do it, striking where the bruises wouldn't show.

He sure had been convincing about where the blame lay—with her. It was *her* fault he got so angry. *Her* fault she wasn't the kind of wife he expected her to be. *Her* fault she got hurt. And she believed him. She'd burned every bridge she had by quitting her job and distancing herself from her friends, too ashamed to let them know what her life had become.

"The hell you are," Lucy shot back. "I have the

police reports and photos that will keep you from ever getting your hands on her."

"Lucy, watch your language," her mother admonished, her pale, watery eyes pleading. "Have some respect for your husband."

Nadine had been a beauty once. Lucy used to love looking at pictures of her mother before she'd married her father. Living with Larry had chewed Nadine up from the inside out. Covering for him and pretending nothing was wrong had worn away her softness, leaving behind a woman on the edge of brittle. The invisible nicks and scars from years of abuse had whittled her down to the point where Lucy hardly recognized her mother as the person in those old photos.

I could've been her. I almost was her.

"I have your mother's blessing and a new lawyer who's a shark. You don't stand a chance against me."

Lucy looked at her mother and knew what Kevin said was true. Nadine had been harping on Lucy to get back together with Kevin so that Poppy could have a real family, not a broken one. Her mother had always been the keep-the-family-together type. No matter how many times Nadine's husband, Larry, had come home drunk reeking of perfume and alcohol, Nadine always put him to bed as if he was the long-lost king come home.

Now Kevin had charmed Nadine just the way Larry had. She didn't see past the good looks and good manners to the soul of the man who'd nearly put her own daughter in the hospital more than once. It had taken Lucy too long to realize that by marrying Kevin she'd repeated her mother's history. That wasn't what she wanted for *her* daughter or for herself.

"I will fight you with everything I have in me," Lucy swore. "You are not taking my daughter anywhere, and you are certainly not leaving the state with her."

Kevin's eyes went cold, and his hands balled into fists the way they always did right before he struck her. Lucy standing up to him was new, and she could tell he didn't like it. If her mother wasn't in the room, Lucy would be on the floor.

Poppy was sobbing now. Lucy patted her back and tried to soothe her, but her own insides were a tangled mass. She believed Kevin. He *would* take her daughter by any means, and he would make Lucy pay for her insolence.

"She's my daughter too," Kevin said. "You're gone all day working. Nadine is a terrific grandma, but Poppy needs a mother. She needs to be cared for in her own home, not shuttled back and forth between caregivers. My wife—"

"And which wife would that be, hmm? Wife number one or two? Maybe it's wife number three."

"She doesn't mean that, Kevin." Nadine had the nerve to back him and not her own daughter. And then she took it further, making Lucy the bad guy here. "He's your husband. I know you've gone through some rough times—"

"Rough times? He has three wives. And he beat me, mother. *Beat me.*"

Nadine worried her hands, glancing from Kevin to Lucy and back again. "Lucy, please. Listen to him. I know the two of you could work things out if you'd just be a little more understanding."

"I've cleared my legal troubles. I know I wasn't always the best husband to you, Lucy, but I love you, and I want to make it work with you. Maybe go to counseling. I want us to be a family again. I'll do anything to get you back, Lucy. Anything."

"You see," Nadine continued. "He loves you."

Lucy knew he meant it too. He would do anything to get her back, including turning her mother against her and taking her daughter from her. She'd never be free of him, free from his threats. He would keep chasing her like he'd chased her from room to room of their house, hitting and screaming at her. It would never stop.

"No." Lucy gripped her daughter tighter. It wasn't going to work this time. He wasn't going to sweet-talk her into forgiving him as she'd done too many times before. "Get out." She pointed at the door. "Get out right now!"

She'd hidden the worst from her mother, from everyone. And then she'd gotten her and her daughter out of that hellhole. She was never going back, and she sure as hell was never going to let her daughter be raised in a home like the one she grew up in.

"This is my house, and I say who stays and who goes," Nadine said.

"Fine." Lucy shook, her face hot, her heart racing. "I'll leave." She grabbed Poppy's diaper bag from the chair and headed for the door.

"This isn't the last of it," Kevin threatened. "I will be

back for Poppy and for you. I want my family with me, and I always get what I want, Lucy. Remember that."

Lucy ran down the front steps as though Kevin would reach out and rip Poppy from her arms. She believed him. He'd do anything to get what he wanted.

She bundled Poppy into her car seat and then took off down the street without buckling her own belt. It wasn't until she got to the light and checked her rearview mirror that she put her seat belt on. She almost expected to find Kevin in his car behind her. It had been more than six months since she'd seen him, and he terrified her more now than when she'd been with him. She knew what it would be like to go back. How small her and Poppy's world would be.

There was no way she was ever going to let her daughter grow up the way she had. Walking in on her father screwing the next-door neighbor on their dining room table and the beating she'd gotten from him not to tell. It wouldn't have mattered if she'd told her mother or not. Nadine wouldn't have believed her and would've punished her for lying. Lucy was always the one who paid to keep their family together.

Until the night when Lucy was fourteen and Larry had been killed in a car accident that was entirely his fault. Two other people died that night because Larry got drunk and decided to drive to see his girlfriend in Garland. After that it was just Lucy and her mother, who never really got over the loss of the husband she adored.

That was when Lucy started spending afternoons with her maternal grandma, Poppy, who she adored so much she'd named her daughter after her. Baby Poppy even had strawberry-blonde hair like her namesake.

At a light, Lucy glanced back at her daughter in her car seat. She'd fallen asleep with her finger in her mouth and tears still clinging to her eyelashes. The sight just about broke Lucy's heart. She'd done her best to care for her precious baby and support them financially. Her best wasn't good enough. She was faced with losing their apartment because she couldn't afford the raise in rent next month, and she couldn't afford to move. Kevin was back threatening to take Poppy away, and now she'd lost the only babysitter she could afford on her salary—her mother.

As if sensing Lucy was nearly to her breaking point, both the check-engine light and gas light came on at the same time. She dropped her head on the steering wheel and burst into tears.

CAL POURED HIMSELF A WHISKEY NEAT, propped his bare feet on his desk in his home office, and turned on the TV to the business report. He turned the volume up to drown out the rain beating against the windows. This was the way he wound down most of his days. He hadn't been the hell-raiser the local papers accused him of being for several years now, but that didn't mean he'd lost the title. Once pigeonholed, the press seemed to look for ways to make it stick. Especially when you were as successful and rich as Cal was.

Oh, he'd more than earned his reputation—had the

tattoo on his ass to prove it—but he wasn't that guy anymore. There'd been a time when he'd thought up ways to get in the newspaper or on TV. When his business had been as young as he was. But he knew better now, made better choices, and had grown his business empire into something he could be proud of.

The *Pleasure at Home* shopping show for adult toys had started out as a lark, a way to snub his nose at conventional business. He owned the TV station, why not put whatever he wanted on it? Over the years it had grown into a very steady, very lucrative source of income.

And that was how he'd met Lucy. He couldn't help grinning at the memory even now. The first time he'd seen her she was tail up in an exceptionally short skirt, trying to find something under the couch on the set for *Pleasure at Home*. Rounded hips, rounded ass, and long legs that ended in stilettos. She'd popped up, flipping back her long blonde hair, holding a vibrating bullet that had slipped out of one of the products.

Pink cheeked with a wide smile, she'd stolen his breath like a mule kick to the chest. And then she'd spoken, asking him if he'd enjoyed the view. She'd called him cowboy with a wink and adjusted her skirt, and he didn't think he'd ever seen a woman more beautiful in his life.

After that he'd set about trying to woo her, breaking his number-one rule—he didn't date, mess with, or sleep with his employees. Ever. But as soon as he'd laid eyes on Lucy he'd wanted to do every single one of those things with her, personal rule be damned.

It had taken nearly two years and a lot of effort, but he'd eventually won her over. The next couple of months had been the most interesting, frustrating, and exciting of his entire life. Then he'd gone and screwed everything up. He'd tried to tell her he was sorry, that it was a stupid, careless mistake, but Lucy would have nothing to do with his explanations or with him after that.

He only had himself to blame. After years of cultivating a debauched reputation and allowing the rumors about him to go unanswered, he'd paid the price and lost Lucy. When she'd stumbled into his office today, he couldn't help but feel like maybe this was the redemption he'd earned by trying to reinvent himself ever since she'd walked out.

He swirled the last swallow of whiskey around in his glass and then downed it in one burning gulp. If she wasn't going to take him up on his offer, he'd have to find another way back into her life.

The doorbell rang, startling him out of his thoughts. Whoever it was had bypassed his front gate. Very few of his friends had the gate code and the kind of relationship with him that they could come over unannounced. Must be his good friend Lucas Vega, dropping by with a report on Lucy's ex. Lucas's security firm was the only one he trusted with this kind of job. It had to be bad news for him to show up at—Jesus— nearly ten o'clock at night in the pouring rain.

Cal turned on the porch light and opened the door to a sight he'd never thought he'd see again—Lucy, here, at his home. She was soaked, her hair and clothes plastered to her. How long had she been standing there? Her eyes were red-rimmed and swollen as if she'd been crying. Her car idled in the drive behind her. Whatever she'd come for, she wasn't staying.

She lifted her chin and flipped the wet strands of her hair back over one shoulder. Damn if she wasn't beautiful, standing there dripping on his porch, defeated yet defiant.

"All right," she said, lip quivering. "I'll marry you."

3

Lucy turned and started back down the steps away from him. This was wrong. This was all wrong.

"Lucy, wait."

She wouldn't wait, she kept on going, and so he followed her barefoot out into the rain.

"Hold up." He got to her just as she reached for the handle of her car door and gripped her arm to keep her from opening it. "What's wrong? What happened?"

She jerked out of his grasp and spun around to face him. "I said I'd marry you. What more do you want?"

"I want to know what's got you so upset."

"Does it really matter?"

"Hell yes, it matters."

"There wasn't anything in your offer that said we had to confide in each other. I agreed to your terms. You're going to get what you want—a wife—isn't that enough?"

He reached for her again. She flinched as though

he'd hit her. *What the hell?* He put his palms up to show he wouldn't try to touch her. She crossed her arms over her chest and glared at him, clearly embarrassed at her overreaction.

Something or someone had her spooked, and he'd bet it had to do with her son-of-a-bitch ex. He took half a step back and gentled his tone. "Come inside and dry off. Let's talk about this."

She looked for a moment like she might agree, glancing up at the house and then back at him. "It's late, and I already said all I came to say."

"Where would you like to do it?"

"Do what?"

"Get married. And when? We need to set a date."

"Does it matter? This is all your deal." She paused, looking away and then back. "Soon. I think it should be soon."

"Okay. We can do it as soon as you like. Why don't you come inside, and we can work it out?"

"Poppy's supposed to be asleep. It's past her bedtime."

"I'd like to meet her. Show her where she'll be living."

"She's only eight months old. She's not going to be impressed by how lavish your house is."

He cracked a half smile. She was starting to sound more like the Lucy he knew.

"Well, I don't know. She might think the new media room is kinda cool."

"And you think she's gonna care how big your screen is?"

"Maybe. I've been told it's quite impressive."

Her laugh rumbled through him, deep throated and so damn sexy. "All right. I guess we can come in for a little while."

"Hang on. Stay right there." He jogged up the front steps and grabbed an umbrella from the stand just inside the front door. Returning, he was relieved to find she hadn't moved.

He popped open the umbrella. "For Poppy," he explained. "So she doesn't get wet."

She eyed him as though she was trying to decide if he was for real or not. Again he wondered what the hell had happened with her since he'd seen her earlier that day. Whatever it was had driven her to him, and for that he couldn't help but feel grateful. At the same time it pissed him off. Someone had messed with her.

He held the umbrella over her as she unhooked the baby from her seat. She wrapped her in a blanket and reached for a big bag, which he took from her. He walked up the steps with her, protecting them from the rain. Motioning her into the house, he followed her inside. He dealt with the umbrella and closed the door to find her examining him like there was something wrong with him, but she couldn't make out what it was.

"Go on in to the living room. I'll grab some towels and be right back."

He waited until she started that direction to run upstairs. She looked so lost he wasn't sure if she'd stay or bolt. He made it back downstairs in record time, out of breath and glad to find her standing in the middle of the room as though she wasn't sure what to do with herself.

He set the towels on the coffee table. "Here you go." He held his arms out. "I'll hold her while you dry off."

"Do you even know how to hold a baby?"

"Of course I do. I even know how to change a diaper."

"Don't tell me you've got a secret baby holed up somewhere."

"Hell no. My parents are foster parents, and they frequently get babies to care for. I know my way around babies as well as you do I'd imagine."

He could tell she didn't believe him, but she handed him the baby anyway, watching all the while to make sure he didn't drop her. He easily repositioned Poppy so she wasn't pressed against his wet shirt. He moved the edge of the blanket back and got his first look at her. She resembled Lucy so much it blew him away. Except for the red hair. Where had that come from?

"Her hair is red," he blurted out.

"Just like my grandma's. Are you sure you're okay there?"

"We're fine." He stood there staring down at Poppy who stared right back. And then she smiled at him, and damned if she wasn't the most perfect baby he'd ever seen. "She likes me better than you do."

Lucy glanced up from rubbing the water out of her hair to find Cal and Poppy grinning at each other. He looked so strange and yet so right, standing there soaking wet, holding her baby, that it made her chest pinch. If things had gone differently between them,

Poppy might have had him for a father instead of Kevin. She blotted at the sudden tears that sprang to her eyes, disguising the gesture as checking for mascara smudges.

"Well, hello there, sweet pea. You're as pretty as your momma, aren't you?" Cal's low, honeyed voice made Poppy giggle. He was devastating to ladies of any age.

"You'll flirt with any female."

"Nah, just the good-looking ones."

And that right there had her worrying she'd made a mistake in coming here and agreeing to marry Cal. He'd earned his bad-boy reputation honestly. She'd been hurt by him before. She couldn't bare the thought of him hurting Poppy as well if she got too attached to him. What was she thinking, bringing a new person into her daughter's life who not only wouldn't go the distance, but could potentially disappoint her? This was going to be a disaster.

But what choice did she have?

She must have traipsed back and forth in the rain between Cal's front door and her car about eighty times, mumbling to herself like a crazy person, before she'd gotten up the nerve to knock. Once she had it was like someone had popped an invisible balloon inside of her filled with tension and apprehension. Maybe this wouldn't be the disaster she expected it to be. Maybe they could keep everything businesslike and cordial and in a year's time she'd be on her way with enough money socked away that she could move her and Poppy as far away from Kevin as possible.

She dried herself off as best she could, all the while keeping a sharp eye on Cal. He was good with Poppy, so natural. He hadn't talked much about his family when they were together. But then they hadn't done much more than screw each other's brains out every chance they got. Talking had pretty much been limited to *your place or mine?*

When she was sure she was as dry as she was going to get, she walked over to the sofa where Cal sat with her daughter. He seemed completely oblivious to how his wet clothes would ruin the leather. But then he could just buy himself a new one the way other people replaced holey socks.

Lucy held her hands out. "I can take her now."

"We're fine. Want a drink?"

"I want my daughter." She still wasn't over Kevin's threat, she realized. It was as though Kevin hung in the air above her, waiting to snatch Poppy away the moment she turned her back.

"Sure." Cal gave Poppy over, eyeing Lucy like she was the one who might disappear. "Want a drink, something to warm you up?"

"That would be nice. Thanks."

Cal rose and went over to the bar in the corner. He moved with the grace and power of a predator. Long and lean, his body never ceased to draw her attention and every other woman's in the room. She'd been so proud to be with him, thinking herself something special. Now she was going to be his wife.

"Why me?" she asked, sitting down and adjusting Poppy in her lap.

He turned with two tumblers half full of amber liquid in each hand. He offered her the one with ice. She couldn't help but be surprised that he remembered how she liked her drink.

He sat next to her on the sofa. "I'm assuming you're asking me why I asked you to marry me."

"I wouldn't put it like that. You didn't really ask me. It was more of an offer like you'd put on a house or a car. But yeah, why me and not, well, *anyone* else?"

"Oh, shit." He set his glass on the table with a thunk. "Hold on. Don't move. I'll be right back."

She followed him out of the room with her gaze. He was acting so strangely tonight. But then this whole thing was strange, from the way he'd made his proposal to the way she'd accepted.

He came back into the room and headed straight for her, and then he did the most astonishing thing— he dropped to one knee in front of her. He took the glass from her and clasped her hand between both of his.

"What are you doing?" She couldn't help the panic in her voice. And she really wished she had three hands so she could knock back that drink.

"Lucy Monroe, would you do me the honor of becoming my wife?"

"What are you doing? Get up."

"Not till you give me an answer."

"I already said I'd marry you. This isn't necessary."

"Yes, it is. Now are you going to give me an answer or not?" He actually looked kind of nervous.

"This isn't real. None of this is real. What are you

trying to do here?" Get her hopes up? Make her feel as though this was the beginning of a real engagement that would become a real marriage? This was insane. *He* was insane.

"It's as real as this." He reached into his pocket and pulled out a small, signature blue box, and her heart rate doubled. Then he lifted the lid, and she thought her heart might stop altogether. The most beautiful cushion cut diamond surrounded by sapphires winked up at her.

"I don't understand." She flipped the box lid closed, unable to stand how incredibly perfect the ring was. "This doesn't make any sense. Why are you doing this?"

"We need a story to tell people. How you came over and we were sitting here having a quiet night in during a rainstorm and then I proposed and you accepted. Only you haven't done your part yet." He opened the box again. "If you don't like the ring, we can exchange it."

Poppy made a grab for the ring, which Lucy blocked just in time.

"Well, Poppy seems to like it. Don't you, sweet pea?" He tweaked Poppy's nose, making her giggle. "Are you going to make me stay down here until my legs go numb?" he asked Lucy.

Lucy stared at the ring, which was so dang beautiful it made her eyes water.

"Oh, damn, darlin'. Don't cry. You hate it. I get it." He snapped the lid closed. "We'll get you another one."

"No, you big dumb cowboy. I love it, but I can't accept it."

"Why not?"

"I can't answer your question until you answer mine. Why me?"

"I trust you."

Well, it wasn't poetry or flowers, but it was something he never gave idly. And he'd answered quick enough that she believed him. She supposed it was enough. It wasn't like she expected him to profess his undying love for her. She never would've believed it anyway.

She slowly stuck her left hand out. "Then yes, I will marry you."

He reopened the box and took the ring out. Poppy made another swipe for it, but he slipped it on Lucy's finger before the baby could get a hold of it. It fit perfectly, and her eyes started filling up all over again.

"God, darlin', you're killing me with those tears." He swiped the tear that escaped down her cheek with the pad of his thumb, following it with a kiss. "It won't be so bad, I promise. You might actually like being married to me."

She sniffed, waving his words away. "No, it's not that. I just can't believe what we're going to do. It's crazy."

"It is. It's completely insane."

"While we're talking about crazy, improbable things, do you think it would be okay if Poppy and I move in here before the wedding? My lease is up at the end of the month, and it doesn't really make sense for me to pay the extra expense of a month-to-month lease. You know, if we're going to be married soon."

She held her breath. This was too much to ask. It was a complete betrayal of his trust not telling him the real reason she needed a new place to live. But the fact was, she was too ashamed to tell him how bad things were for her. She'd lost the only babysitter she could afford, which meant she couldn't go to work tomorrow. And she couldn't look for a new job without someone to watch Poppy. Not to mention she'd be homeless at the end of the month.

"That's next week," he said, still on bended knee.

"Yes, I know." She shook her head. "It's okay. Never mind. I'll make it work."

"No. It's fine. You can move in whenever you like."

She let out a heavy, relieved breath. "Thank you. That's very generous of you."

"Now I have a question for you." He grabbed his drink and stood up. "Why did *you* agree to marry *me*?"

h, yes. He would ask that. Nothing was ever easy or taken at face value with Cal. He always looked at cause and effect. He hadn't gotten to where he was in business without examining things from every angle before coming to a decision or making a commitment. She supposed she should've been relieved he took the same care in his personal life, however impersonal this marriage really was.

He'd opened his home to her in her most desperate time. Whatever he was getting out of this marriage, she was getting far more. It wouldn't be fair not to let him know exactly what he was getting himself into. She only hoped he wouldn't back out once he learned just how screwed up her life was and how much of it she was bringing to his doorstep.

"Well," she began. "I need the money. If I could find a job with the same pay, hours, and perks, I'd take it."

He swallowed a rather large amount of his drink. "No doubt."

"I recently lost my babysitter, so I'll have to look for a new one right away. Which brings up another question—when will I start getting paid?"

"Don't worry about it."

"Well, see, I kind of need to. Without someone to watch Poppy, I can't go in to work tomorrow." She hated how reedy and needy her voice sounded.

He refilled his drink and then hers. She hadn't realized she'd drained the glass.

"Darlin', I'd really appreciate it if you'd get to the part where you answer my question. Why did you agree to marry me?"

She looked down at Poppy, who had fallen asleep with her little fist in her mouth. She'd do anything for her baby. Anything. She gulped back more liquid courage and forged on.

"I'm getting to that."

"Is it all about the money?"

"No."

"Then what's it about? Cuz I've got to tell you, darlin', you look like a woman running from trouble. I think as your husband-to-be I should get a heads up, don't you?"

She went for another swallow only to find her glass empty. He offered her another refill, which she accepted. Admitting to Cal how completely stupid she'd been about everything and throwing herself at his mercy had to be one of the lowest moments of her life. A couple more sips and she might be able to get it all out. As long as she didn't look at him. *Just look at Poppy.*

She drained the glass once more, but this time instead of refilling it, he pried it from her hand and set it on the table.

"My mother would watch Poppy for me while I went to work," she began. "It wasn't the best situation, but she was the only babysitter I could afford. It's hard to turn down free, you know?" She glanced up at him to find him watching her with that Cal intensity that both thrilled and unnerved her.

"What happened with your mother?"

"I was late picking Poppy up. I had to make up the time at work that it took to go into Dallas."

The time it took her to come to his office and ask for her old job back, Cal realized. There was more going on here than losing a babysitter. He believed her that it wasn't all about money. If it took all night, he'd get to the bottom of it.

"When I got to her house," she continued, "there was a car I didn't recognize in the driveway. It was Kevin's."

So this was about her son-of-a-bitch ex. Great.

"He wasn't supposed to be there. But Mother let him in to see Poppy. He doesn't have visitation. To my mother, a family is a unit no matter what. She took his side against me. If I leave Poppy with her, she's going to let Kevin see her."

"Why doesn't he have visitation? Because of his arrest for bigamy?"

"That's partly why. Also he's threatened to take Poppy back to Utah with him. I'm afraid he'll make good on that threat, and if he does, I might never get to see my daughter again."

Something wasn't jiving here. But her fear that her ex would take her baby was very real. She was terrified. It was that terror—way more than the need for money and the flexible-hours bullshit—that had driven her to accept his offer. The disappointment he felt over that revelation surprised him. He knew she hadn't agreed because she loved him or even wanted him. He was literally her last and only resort. But *son of a bitch*. A part of him had hoped she might care for him at least a little.

"That's one of the reasons I asked about moving in early," she admitted. "The gates and security. I promise we'll stay out of your way. You'll hardly know we're here. Poppy's a very good baby. We'll clean up—"

He put a hand up to stop her. "You're not a guest here, Lucy. You're going to be my wife. This is going to be your home as much as mine."

"Okay. I just don't want you to think I'll take advantage."

"Stop acting like I'll kick you and Poppy to the curb for the slightest infraction. As long as you wear my ring, you have a place here." He wanted to add that as long as she wore his ring she had a place in his life *and* his heart, but he didn't think she could handle much more pressure than she was already under.

His instinct told him there was more to the story, something to do with the ex. Maybe the feelers he put out earlier that day would pay off and he'd get a look at the whole picture and know exactly what he was up against.

She shifted Poppy to the couch next to her and adjusted the blanket around her. She was a devoted mother to her daughter. It had occurred to him more than once that Poppy could be his. He and Lucy had certainly been careless more than a time or two. If things had gone differently between them...

She glanced down at the ring on her finger. He'd spent nearly the entire afternoon looking for the right ring, betting against the odds that she'd agree to marry him. Maybe it wasn't fashionable to have colored stones in an engagement ring, but the sapphires reminded him of her eyes. She said she liked it, but she kept staring at it oddly, like it didn't quite fit her.

"Thank you," she said, eyes still on the ring. "I promise I'll do my best to uphold our bargain and be the kind of wife you need me to be."

He grabbed the bottle of whiskey and splashed more into each of their glasses. She was acting like a wounded puppy, and it pissed him off. He wanted the Lucy who went toe-to-toe with him and gave as good as she got. So maybe he'd have to draw that Lucy out.

"What kind of wife do you think I need?" he asked.

"Well," she started and then took a sip. "You said you needed a hostess, someone to hold dinner parties?"

"That's right."

"I'm a fairly good cook, but I think it would probably be best if we had the dinners catered."

"And what about the charity balls? You do know how to dance, don't you?"

"I…ah…know how to sway…"

She finished off her drink, so he refilled her glass. He wondered if she'd realized it yet that she was too drunk to drive home.

"Do you know anything about corporate wives?" he asked.

"I'm not sure if I've met very many."

"And your wardrobe. We're going to have to make some changes. That blouse you're wearing, besides being cut too low—" but not low enough for his taste, "—is too small. I can see half your bra."

She glanced down at her chest, then her head popped up. The fire was back in her eyes just as he intended. "You cannot see half my bra. It gapes a little, but it's not obscene."

"Darlin', from where I'm sitting, my eyes have practically gotten to second base with you. And your skirt—"

"What about my skirt?"

"It's tight enough for when we're at home. Personally the office sex kitten look does a lot for me, but it sends the wrong message to every other man who is *not* your soon-to-be husband."

"Look, I know I've put on some weight—"

"Yeah, and you put it in all the right places. That's what counts." He ran his gaze over her the way he'd been wanting to ever since he'd seen her again this afternoon. She flushed under his gaze. "You're making me want to add an addendum to the option we discussed in my office."

Her gorgeous mouth dropped open for a second and then she rebounded. "You're a pig." She didn't sound half as pissed off as she would've been if she wasn't so intoxicated.

"I can't help it. I'm a male pig. And you, darlin', are very female."

"I have a question about that option." She downed the last of her whiskey and pushed her glass at him for more. He obliged. "How open to options is it?"

"What do you mean?"

"I mean just how many option clauses do you have open?" She was slurring her words now.

"Just the one, darlin'. Just the one."

She tried to point at him, but she couldn't quite focus enough to nail him down with it. "I mean, there's not like a brunette option or a redhead option or even another blonde-headed-ded-ded option, is there? Cuz, I know you. You're a man who likes his options. So if we're gonna get married, I'm gonna have to insist you cut..." she made a slicing motion with her hand and tipped over slightly then recovered, "...all your other options. You get me, cowboy?"

"I get you, darlin'. Yours is the only option for me. But I'm going to want the same assurances from you."

"Psshh." She waved him away. "Between my giant ass and Poppy, there aren't any men who would even give me a second look let alone options." She rolled her eyes, weaving a little, and then finished off her glass.

He took it from her before she could ask for another.

"I seriously doubt that. But just so we're clear on all our options, why don't we write them down." He wanted her to remember this conversation tomorrow.

"Oh! Like a contract. Good idea. And we should have it notarized so there's no weaseling out of it."

He was halfway to grabbing a sheet of paper when her words stopped him. "You want to make our agreement formal?"

"Well, yeah. Sure. Why not? You like binding contracts, don't you?" She giggled. "I know for sure you like binding." She waggled her eyebrows at him.

"You want to put binding in our binding contract?"

She slapped her knee, wide-eyed. "We totally should!"

He sat back down next to her with a pad of paper and a pen and started writing. "So binding is option number one. What's option number two?"

"No, no. Scratch that out. Number one should be the option that says neither one of us doesn't get any other options. Or we're the other's only option. No other optioning. Or something like that. Otherwise I'm not havin' any kind of options with you." She shook her finger at him, then held up three fingers. "Two can be binding. Oh! And we should make three or is it four...I can't remember...but it should definitely be that thing you do with your teeth and your tongue right here." She made a sweeping gesture that encompassed her whole body.

He started writing, jotting down all of the *options* she wanted, adding a few of his own with her permission. When they were done, they had a five-page list of some of the most inventive sexual activities ever compiled.

"Okay. Okay," she said. "I've got one more. This is the last one. I promise."

Somehow when he wasn't looking she'd gotten ahold of the whiskey bottle and refilled her glass... two...no, maybe three times.

"And what would that be?" He really couldn't believe it. She'd outdone anything his imagination could come up with by yards. He couldn't wait to see what she came up with next.

"We need a..." she hiccupped, "...an optional option."

"An optional option. What exactly is that?"

"It's an option that says that all of the options are completely optional." She waved her hands around. "Optionally speaking of course."

"That goes without saying."

She snorted. "Right. That's what *I* thought. Didn't turn out that way." She tapped the page with her finger. "Write it down. I want it in writing this time. Op-tion-al."

He stared at her for a moment, not quite believing what she'd inadvertently told him. What in the hell had her marriage to that asshole been like? Had he forced her to have sex with him? How bad had things gotten for her?

He cleared his throat, which had become inexplicably clogged. "How about: Everything in this option agreement is absolutely and completely optional, and either party can pull their option at any time during any option?"

"Oohhh. That's good."

He wrote it down. "Now what?"

"Now we sign. Wait! No. We need a notoriety to make it all officially official."

"You mean a notary."

"Right." She squinted up at him. "Isn't that what I said?"

"Close enough. Let me make a phone call."

Twenty minutes later they had a signed and notarized option agreement thanks to Cal's business connections. It was going to cost him a couple of hundred dollars extra for the late-night service, but if it made Lucy feel secure in marrying him, then it was money well spent.

He was still trying to wrap his head around what Lucy had let slip. What had she been through in the past seventeen months? Whatever it was had nearly broken her spirit. He was going to have to be extra gentle, extra careful to gain back her trust and make her feel secure again.

He returned from showing the notary out to find Lucy passed out on the couch next to Poppy. He stood in the doorway a moment, watching them, hardly able to believe they were here. His gaze tracked to his ring on Lucy's finger. Twenty-four hours ago if someone had told him that they'd be engaged, he would've laughed in their face. But here she was broken and alone and now his, finally his.

As he bent down and kissed Poppy's then Lucy's cheeks, he swore that they would never again want for anything. As long as he was in their lives, they would never be insecure and afraid.

Lucy woke up with the worst hangover she'd ever had in her life. Or else she was dead and the pain in her head was punishment for all the bad things she'd done. She risked opening her eyes to a dark room she didn't recognize.

Where was she? *Where was Poppy?*

She climbed out of bed faster than she should have, swaying so badly she had to grab the bedpost to keep from falling over. She found the door after three tries—who in the world had two closets in their bedroom?—and stumbled out into the hall. Wait. She knew this house.

Cal's.

Locating the staircase, she made her way downstairs. Last night came back to her in drips and dribbles with each step. Oh my God. Had they really made a sexual option agreement? And had it notarized? No. That couldn't be right. What exactly had she agreed to?

Noises from the kitchen drew her that direction.

She stopped in the doorway, gaping at the unexpected vision that greeted her. A shirtless Cal had Poppy down to her diaper, tied to a chair with a towel, and he was feeding her applesauce. It had to be the strangest, sexiest, and most confusing sight she'd ever seen.

He'd always had a great body, but now... She resisted the urge to fan herself. Holy cow. He must work out every day to get a body like that. Not an ounce of anything except hard, chiseled muscle on him. Da-yam.

It took her a moment to find her voice. "What are you doing?"

Cal looked up at her and grinned. "Breakfast. How are you feeling?" He spooned some applesauce into Poppy's mouth, then held out a bowl of Cheerios for Poppy to feed herself.

"You let me drink too much."

"I cut you off. You snuck more." He turned, running his gaze over her. "There's coffee if you can handle it."

"Ugh. Maybe." She watched as he wiped Poppy's face and hands with a washcloth. "How do you know how to do all this baby stuff?"

"Told you. My parents foster children. Even now when I visit, I'm drafted into diaper duty."

She made her way over to the coffeepot and poured a cup. "Wow. Cal Sellers, the internationally known business mogul, changes diapers and feeds babies. Who would've guessed?"

"I'm a man of many talents, aren't I, Poppy?"

Poppy squealed as he lifted her out of the chair and stood up. Lucy nearly lost her breath. Cal looked so good, so right holding her daughter that she had to bite the inside of her lip to keep from bursting into tears. Kevin had only ever held Poppy if he had to. He'd never fed her or changed a diaper in his life. And here was this man who'd broken her heart—but not nearly as devastatingly as Kevin had—caring for her baby as if she was his own. She'd made many mistakes in her life, but choosing Kevin to help raise her child had to be the biggest, most irreversible mistake she would ever make.

Cal wiggled his nose against Poppy's, making her giggle. Poppy slapped her chubby hands on Cal's cheeks, trying to get him do it again. He did, and Poppy put her head back and laughed harder than Lucy had ever seen her laugh. Cal blew a raspberry on her belly, and she laughed harder. Cal's answering chuckle did funny things to Lucy's insides. Or else it was the coffee mixed with the leftover whiskey in her belly.

"I can take her now," she blurted out.

"What? Nah, we're fine. Go take a shower. I don't have to leave for another half hour." He didn't even look at her. All of his attention was on Poppy.

"About last night..."

Both Cal and Poppy turned to glance at her. "What about it?" he asked.

"I'm not really sure what happened after this." She held up her hand with the engagement ring.

"Besides you getting drunk?"

"Yeah. Besides that."

"And passing out."

"Besides that too. Was there a notary involved?"

"You were rather insistent on that, darlin'. What else could I do but oblige you?"

"Where is it?"

"The option agreement? In the living room."

Why did he seem so totally unconcerned about it? And what exactly did it say?

She set her coffee down, then picked it back up and took it into the living room with her. She had a feeling she was going to need the fortitude it would provide.

Cal followed with Poppy. Lucy found a small stack of pages with Cal's neat block lettering on the coffee table where he'd said it would be. She dropped down on the sofa and leafed through it. It was worse than she thought. Swallowing her panic on a bitter sip of black coffee, she turned to Cal, who was trying to pry Poppy's fingers from his chest hair.

"This, uh, agreement." She held it up. "What exactly does it mean? I'm not, like, bound to any of it or anything, am I? Cuz I'm not exactly sure how number twenty-three would work."

He came over, took the papers from her, and flipped through them. "Me either," he said. "But you insisted I write it down."

"But it's not legal, is it?"

"If you're asking if I'll force you to do any of the naughty things your dirty mind thought up—read the last option." He handed her the agreement back.

She found the last page and read it, then let out the breath she'd been holding. "Oh, thank God."

"We were just joking around." But he didn't sound like he thought it was much of a joke.

"A joke. Right."

"I made a couple of phone calls this morning. The

movers are going to pack up your things day after tomorrow and bring them here. Also, I hired you a nanny. Her name's Sam."

"I don't want a nanny. I can take care of Poppy just fine."

"I know you can, darlin', but I thought you might need some help while you get things settled. The nanny can be here with you while you do that. That way you can get to know her and hopefully like her."

"I don't even get to meet her first? How do you know she's any good? She could be one of those nannies who beat the children they care for."

He gave her a *get real* look. "You really think I wouldn't hire the absolute best?"

"Maybe your best is different than my best."

"Let's go get you dressed, Poppy." He turned to leave the room.

"Cal."

He stopped and glanced back at her.

"I can't leave her with a stranger," Lucy said. "She's just a baby."

"You wouldn't be, darlin'. Sam's going to be here to help you, like I said. If you don't approve of her, we'll find someone else. But trust me on this, you're going to approve." He started out of the room again, then turned back. "By the way, how did you like the room you stayed in last night?"

"What?" Her mind was still stuck on nannies and moving.

"The bedroom. It's the largest one besides mine. If

you don't like it, you can pick a different one, but that would mean we'd have to move Poppy's room too."

"What do you mean Poppy's room? I didn't know she had one."

"The one between yours and mine." He said it like she should've already known.

She rubbed at her pounding forehead. This time yesterday she was nearly homeless and jobless. Twenty-four hours later she was engaged, moving into a mansion, and getting a nanny. Oh, yes. And she'd signed some kind of optional sex contract with her fiancé that may or may not be binding in a court of law.

"Everything's going to be fine, darlin'. Isn't it, Poppy?"

She watched as Cal left the room with her daughter as though they started their day like this every day. She must have upset some kind of space-time continuum when she'd walked into Cal's office yesterday. Nothing since then had been the same. It was all off kilter and out of whack. But other than the ridiculous option agreement, she couldn't think of one single thing she'd change.

And that worried her most of all.

THREE DAYS LATER, Cal sat in his office overlooking the Dallas skyline, contemplating the changes his life had gone through in the past few days. Lucy and Poppy had moved in. Cal and Lucy's engagement had been announced and was big society news. He found himself racing Lucy to get to Poppy when she cried first thing in the morning. He usually won.

Lucy approved of Sam the nanny, who turned out to be a manny. Cal had trusted Lucas to find the perfect nanny/bodyguard for Poppy. He'd grilled Lucas about Sam's qualifications up one side and down the other, but it had never occurred to him to ask if Sam was a man or a woman. He'd assumed. And now there was another man in his house, spending all day alone with Lucy.

Cal hadn't so much as kissed Lucy since that peck on the cheek when she'd cried as he put his ring on her finger. He began to wonder if they'd ever get past option number one in the option agreement. Not that he was complaining. Much. Whatever Lucy had been through was because of him. He was going to have to tread lightly to re-earn her trust.

At least he'd gotten her to set a date for the wedding —a week from Saturday. There wasn't much time to plan. All he really needed was Lucy, a license, and a preacher, but he wanted her to have the wedding she'd always wanted. So he'd hired a wedding planner who was showing Lucy table linens and centerpieces at this very moment. He was supposed to meet them later to look at venues.

Right now he was waiting for his good friend Lucas, who he'd asked to check into some things for him concerning Lucy's ex. Lucas had started his own security company a couple of years ago. He'd met his now-wife Mi when Cal had hired him to be her bodyguard. Lucy and Mi had been hosts of *Pleasure at Home* and good friends until Lucy quit to marry that asshole. The show had done quite well with Mi as host, but in a few months she'd be going out on maternity leave.

Cal wondered if Lucy had confided in Mi about her ex and how much of that had Mi divulged to Lucas. Lucy had been circumspect at best about her ex and downright evasive at worst.

There was a knock at the door, then Lucas opened it and came in, closing it behind him. "Hey."

Cal stood and shook hands with his friend. "Can I offer you anything?"

"I'm good."

"Have a seat." He waited for Lucas to settle in a chair and then tried to act cool as he asked the most important question he might ever ask. "What have you learned about Kevin Walker?"

Lucas shifted in his chair. Not a good sign. Nothing ruffled the six-foot-six, two-hundred-and-seventy-pound former Navy SEAL. Lucas opened the file he'd brought with him. "As you know he was arrested for bigamy eight months ago."

Cal knew it because it was him who had discovered Kevin Walker's other wives. Lucy had been his third wife. Walker had missed Poppy's birth because he was sitting in a jail cell.

"What's happening with those charges?"

"He was released on bond and fled the state. They suspect he might be living with one of his wives in Utah. If convicted, he could get anywhere from two to ten years in jail and a hefty fine." Lucas smirked. "The D.A. would really like to know his whereabouts."

"If I find out, I'll be sure to be a good citizen and let him know."

"Did you know that Lucy has a protective order against him?"

"No. She said that he didn't have any visitation rights, but she didn't say why."

Lucas grunted. "Restraining orders are typically given to victims of violence."

"What are you saying?"

Lucas pulled a stack of photos out of the file and laid them on the desk in front of Cal. At first he wasn't quite sure of what he was looking at, and then it came at him like a bullet, punching a hole into his chest and knocking him back into his seat. He flipped through the photos, the sick knot in his belly growing. They'd been taken at different times he realized. How could this be? What kind of sick bastard did this to a woman? He swallowed the bile rising up the back of his throat.

"How many times?" he managed to ask.

"Seven are documented here," Lucas said quietly. "There are notes on several more. There was one brief hospitalization. For a burn."

"Why isn't this asshole in jail?"

"First conviction carries a small fine. There are charges pending on a second case that could include jail time and a bigger fine. It's messed up, but the penalty for having more than one legal wife is heftier than beating your wife nearly unconscious."

"Jesus fucking Christ. He better hope I never set eyes on him."

"He better hope neither of us does."

Cal handed the photos back to Lucas. "Find him."

"Already on it. The lead about the rental car was a good one. He rented it under an alias that we can track if he uses it again."

"I wanted to talk to you about the security at my house. It's not adequate enough."

Lucas handed him a second folder. "My proposal. Besides the nanny, what other security personnel would you like to add?"

"Yeah, and thank you for that. That's just what I wanted, another man around my fiancée."

"He's British Special Forces with a certificate from a highly exclusive English nanny school. I'd trust him to guard my own kid."

Cal gave his friend a dirty look. "Yeah, I'll believe it when you hire him to hang around Mi all day. He sings and plays guitar like a fucking rock star. Plus he's got an accent. I can't get a word in between all of the praise Lucy heaps on this guy."

Lucas had the balls to laugh at his predicament. "Yeah, but does a rock star know over a hundred ways to kill with his bare hands? He's the best I've got. What's better than a ninja nanny?"

"I'm not sure that helps."

"He's been married nearly ten years. Besides that, he's a professional. My guys don't fuck around, or they don't have a job."

"That helps. Got any gardener ninjas or cooking ninjas? Maybe a hot-maid ninja? I could use some of those."

Lucas rose. "I'll see what I can do." He headed for the door.

"One more thing."

Lucas turned back. "Yeah?"

Cal came around the desk. "Will you stand up with me at my wedding?"

"Yeah, man." Lucas held out his hand, and Cal shook it. "I'd be glad to."

Cal clapped him on the back. "That means you're in charge of the bachelor party. Make it good. And by good I mean poker and booze."

"I thought for a minute you were going to say strippers."

"Only if you've got a ninja stripper on your payroll."

"I'll look around for one."

Cal showed his friend out, then went back to barely noticing the view outside his window. Lucy filled his thoughts. Those photos... Goddamn. He'd never get those images out of his head, the cuts, the bruises, the bite marks, and other damage he couldn't tell how it had been caused. He scrubbed his hands over his face. She'd lived through hell and had somehow gotten away. She'd run to him when she had no one else.

He would do anything for her, but the thing she needed from him most was to be safe. In that, he wouldn't let her down.

6

Lucy stared at her reflection in the dressing-room mirror, hardly recognizing herself. The hairstylist had rolled and twisted her hair into a half-up, half-tumbling-down style that was both chaste and scandalous. The makeup artist had done something to her skin that made it glow and had even managed to cover her scar so that both of her shoulders appeared smooth and flawless. The last thing she wanted today was a reminder of the damage her last marriage had done to both her body and heart. Kevin had been drunk when he'd burned her or else he'd never have left so permanent a mark.

Her silk wedding dress was also a contradiction with a strapless, sweetheart neckline, flowered belt, and A-line skirt. It left some parts exposed and others chastely covered. She felt...beautiful. For the first time in seventeen long months she wasn't worried about repercussions for a skirt that was too short or for makeup that was too garish.

She hoped Cal liked the way she looked.

"Here." Mi handed her the pearl earrings she'd given Lucy as a wedding gift. They perfectly matched the string of pearls Cal had gotten Lucy as his gift.

"Are you sure you want to marry him?" Mi asked. "You have other options, you know."

No. She didn't. She didn't have any options, but she wasn't about to confess this to Mi after keeping what Kevin had done to her a secret for so long. The shame of it was always there, always hovering over her. Speaking of it was more than she could face because if she said the words, the enormity of every-thing she'd been through would come crashing down over her.

"I know this is going to sound a little crazy," Lucy said. "But I want to marry him."

She did, she realized. The doubts were there, hovering in the background, ghosts from her previous marriage. She mentally flicked them away. Cal wasn't Kevin. She knew this. She was doing the right thing for both her and Poppy.

"That does sound crazy. Are you very sure? You and Poppy deserve the best."

"And you don't think Cal is the best?"

"I don't think Cal has a full grasp on what's happening here. He's about to become a husband and a father all on the same day. This isn't a merger or acqui-sition, this is a family."

"I know you don't like him—"

"With good reason. He cheated on you. With his secretary. It would be laughable if it wasn't so tragic.

Are you sure you can trust him? Are you sure you want to?"

"Honestly? No. But this isn't what it was before. We're not involved that way. I'm walking into this with wider eyes. Every time I start to soften towards him, the image of him bending his honey over his desk pops up, and my heart hardens all over again. Besides, you and Lucas have enough changes to deal with without taking in a homeless friend and her daughter." Lucy rubbed her friend's gently swollen belly. "Are you going to tell me what you're having, or are you and Lucas keeping it a secret?"

"It's a boy."

Lucy threw her hands up and hugged her friend. "I'm so thrilled for you. For both of you. But my Lord is that going to be a big baby. Lucas is such a big guy."

"Ugh. Don't remind me. And whatever you do, don't remind Lucas. He's freaking out about it."

The wedding planner popped her head in the door. "Five minutes!" Then she popped back out again.

"Okay, this is it," Lucy said. "How do I look?"

Tears appeared in Mi's eyes. "Really beautiful. He's a lucky man, even if he doesn't know it."

"Don't cry. You'll make me cry and my mascara will run."

Mi dabbed at her eyes. "Let's go get you hitched."

∾

LUCY CARRIED her daughter unescorted up the aisle to Cal. He stood so tall and straight in his black tuxedo under the wisteria-draped gazebo. Lucas stood to his left and Mi and the minister to his right. The way Cal stared at Lucy nearly stopped her in her tracks, then made her want to run up the aisle toward him. Her cheeks heated under his gaze. She almost forgot this wasn't a real marriage. She needed to remember this was a business arrangement and nothing more.

And she could do that...when she wasn't looking at him. If she glanced at Mi or the minister or stared just past Cal's shoulder, she could remember that none of this was real. It was all for show. But then her gaze would be drawn to his and she'd be sucked into its tractor beam, imagining that this was the wedding she'd always wanted to the man she'd dreamed of with their future stretched out before them.

But it wasn't.

She repeated after the minister. Listened while Cal pledged his life and love to her. Held out her hand for Cal to place the thin platinum band on her finger. Put her ring on Cal's finger. Said "I do." Heard Cal say it too. And then he lifted her veil. She stared up at him, and the panic hit her sideways. She struggled to keep her feet planted and not run back down the aisle. He leaned toward her, and she closed her eyes, going to that empty place in her head where no one and nothing could touch her.

He kissed her briefly and that was it. It was over, and he was holding her hand, leading her back down the aisle. She'd done it. She was married. All that was left was the party, and then she'd be alone with Cal. Her husband.

Accepting the well wishes of the guests was easy. She'd pasted on enough fake smiles as one of the faces of *Pleasure at Home* that it came automatically. Sam had taken Poppy, so she could carry out her duties as Mrs. Cal Sellers. Cal stood at her side, frequently touching her—on the small of her back, across her shoulders, around her waist—branding her as his.

She tried not to think about tonight even as their guests reminded her with good-natured winks and elbows to the side. Would Cal expect there to be a true wedding night, especially after creating the option agreement? Everything he'd said and done told her he wouldn't, but he was a man. A man who went through women the way most went through socks.

She suddenly felt self-conscious, tugging at the top of her dress. What had she been thinking, wearing something so revealing? Even if the dress had made her feel more beautiful than she'd felt in months, maybe years.

The last guest passed through the receiving line, leaving Lucy alone with Cal.

"How about some champagne?" he asked.

Alcohol. "I'd love some."

He took her hand and led her toward the head table set up at the front of the room. On the way, he snagged two flutes of champagne and handed one to her. She had to concentrate on not downing the entire glass at once. It had occurred to her more than once that if this wedding had taken place seventeen months ago, she would've been the happiest bride who ever wore Vera Wang. But now she stood beside her handsome husband surrounded by mostly strangers and wished that the earth would open up and swallow her whole. Or else that she could drown herself and her memories of her previous marriage in enough champagne that she'd be too sick to think about what came next.

Cal watched Lucy out of the corner of his eye. She was so pale her blue eyes were nearly black. And she gulped the hundred-dollar-a-bottle champagne like it was air and she was under water...drowning. When she drained it, he handed her a glass of water. She was not getting drunk tonight. She was going to be completely sober for their first night as husband and wife. To ensure that, he excused himself and gave a whispered order to the head waiter that his wife was to only be given alcohol-free beverages.

When he returned, Lucy gave him her stage smile, her gaze passing over him as though he was part of the scenery. He'd had just about enough of Lucy trying to endure what should've been a fun evening.

"You know what I think?" he asked.

"Hmm?"

"I think we need to test out your swaying skills."

"What?"

He held out his hand to her. "May I have this dance?"

She stared at it as if it would strike her, then slowly placed her hand in his. He drew her up and out onto the crowded dance floor. Holding her close, but not as close as he'd like, he danced with his wife for the first time. After a few moments her shoulders relaxed.

"Have I told you how beautiful you look?" he whispered in her ear.

She shook her head.

"You are. Absolutely stunning. I don't think there's a set of eyes that hasn't been on you since you came up the aisle."

"Oh, I don't think—"

"It's true. You're beautiful, darlin'. More beautiful than I deserve, that's for sure."

"Don't be ridiculous."

"Thank you for marrying me."

She looked up at him, surprised. "That was our deal."

"Yeah, but that doesn't mean I'm not grateful." She didn't respond so he pressed on. "I think we're going to get along very well." Still nothing. "You know if we swayed like this every day, we might end up trying some of those options."

"Wouldn't you like that."

"I'm pretty sure you'd like it too. If memory serves, you especially liked number six. The first time we tried it you made this sound that reminded me of—"

She slapped his chest. "Ssh! Keep your voice down."

"That's exactly what I said the first time we tried it. We were in the bathroom at that bistro downtown that you were crazy about—"

"Cal Sellers, if you say another word..."

"You'll what? Do number sixty-four to me? Cuz I might be into some of that with you, darlin'."

"Have you memorized the entire agreement?" She sounded scandalized and kind of turned on too.

"Just my favorite numbers. Tell me about some of yours. What are your favorites?"

"This isn't exactly—"

"This is our wedding, darlin'. And we're slow dancing to our favorite song—"

"This isn't my favorite song."

"It wasn't mine either until about two minutes ago when you started rubbing your body against mine and calling it 'dancing'. Feels more like foreplay than dancing to me."

"Cal!"

"Tell me your top ten favorite options on the option agreement and I'll stop."

"No."

"Top eight."

"No."

"Five and I'll throw in a glass of champagne."

"Two glasses and a promise that you won't smash the cake in my face."

"You have a deal, darlin'."

"Number two." A pale pink blush crept up her chest to her neck, making him want to lick its path.

"The binding option. Good choice. Me or you?"

"You."

"Also an excellent choice. Which others?"

"Seventeen."

"*Really?* Now I wouldn't've expected that from a woman dressed in virginal white, but who am I to argue?"

"Forty-nine, but I think one of those beds with the

head and feet that go up and down would be essential in making it successful."

"I agree." Did she even realize how lovely she was, blushing like a nun watching a porno flick? Or how much he wanted to do every option she'd put into their agreement with her...for her?

"Sixty-three."

He clenched his teeth from groaning out loud. Sixty-three had been one of the few suggestions he'd offered. "I can't argue with you. One more."

She was quiet for a long moment, her tongue sweeping once, twice across her bottom lip. This was the one. The one she really wanted to try. He could tell by the way her gaze darted away and the fact that she'd left it for last. That was his Lucy, always thinking of herself last.

"Thirty."

He did groan then. "Jesus God almighty, darlin', are you trying to make me embarrass myself right here in front of our friends and family?"

"You'd consider thirty?"

"Consider it? I've been dreaming of it practically all my adult life." He was so looking up number thirty when they got back to the house. Whatever it was, he was going to figure out a way to do it better than anyone had ever done it before. She'd be talking about it to her friends for years to come as the end all be all of sexual fantasies fulfilled.

When they got that far. If they ever got that far. First he had to get her to stop looking at him like he'd turn on her at any moment.

"You've never done number thirty?"

"No. And please tell me you have, darlin', so you can teach it to me and I won't feel so inept."

"No. I haven't."

"Then I guess we'll have to learn it together. Someday," he added, so she wouldn't think he had any plans for them other than this moment. "That's five options, and I now owe you a glass of champagne. Shall we?" He held out his elbow for her to take and led her off the dance floor.

The rest of the night went by in a blur of obligatory socializing and wedding traditions. They danced twice more, but neither compared to their first dance as man and wife. Cal couldn't wait to get Lucy out of there and all to himself. He'd booked the honeymoon suite at the Ritz-Carlton for their wedding night. He'd also arranged for Sam to take Poppy.

One night. He'd get one night to show her what marriage to him would really be like. One night.

7

Her wedding night.

Lucy followed her new husband into the suite at the Ritz-Carlton, dread heavy in her belly. The honeymoon suite. He must be expecting her to fulfill her duties as his wife. He'd said everything between them would be optional. He'd even signed a notarized agreement to that effect. But she knew from experience that men didn't always mean what they said when it came to sex. And they didn't always take no for an answer.

Cal had booked this suite. In this fancy hotel. On their wedding night. If that didn't have unspoken expectations all over it, she didn't know what did.

"Are you hungry?" he asked. "I don't know about you, but all I've eaten tonight is that piece of cake you fed me."

Her stomach rumbled as if on cue. "I'm starving."

He found the room service menu and started

leafing through it. "I could eat one of everything. What sounds good to you?"

"A cheeseburger. With fries."

"You got it. Why don't you get changed while I order? Your bags should already be in your room."

Her room. That meant they weren't... He wasn't expecting... She wasn't sure if she was grateful or disappointed. It was a confusing set of emotions that knocked together inside her like stress-ball clackers.

"Which one's mine?" she asked.

"The master. Whichever that one is. Hi," he said into the phone. "I'd like to order some food."

Lucy wandered off toward a set of double doors that had to be the master bedroom. It was and the bed was huge. And was that...? She rushed forward. A Jacuzzi right in the middle of the bedroom with a view of the Dallas skyline. How romantic. Except this wasn't a romance.

"I'm looking forward to that," Cal said from over her shoulder, making her jump and squeak. "Sorry, darlin'. Didn't mean to startle you."

"No, that's okay. It's just that this carpet is so plush it totally absorbed your steps." And now she sounded like an idiot.

"I told Hazel to pack you a bathing suit." He pointed at the Jacuzzi. "Right there is where I plan to have a drink and soak with my wife after dinner."

He gazed at her like she really was his wife and he had all kinds of husbandly plans. She peered inside the Jacuzzi. It looked like heaven. Lots of jets and places to put your feet up. She risked a glance up at Cal, but he'd already turned away and was walking out the door. What in the...?

Hot, cold, hot, cold. Right when she thought she had him and this—whatever it was between them— sorted out, he'd throw her a curve and do the exact opposite of what she expected. He flirted with her like he used to, only it was just words, no action. He'd kissed her exactly twice since she'd walked into his office almost two weeks ago. The one time in his office and then again when the minister had told him that he could now kiss his bride. Three times if she counted the peck on the cheek he'd given her when they got engaged. He'd progressed to hand holding and an arm around her shoulders or a hand at the small of her back in the past week or so but no further.

It was almost as though they were virginal high schoolers with their first crush. She half-expected him to ask her to prom. Well, she guessed their wedding was sort of prom like. She was in a big dress and they'd danced... And now they were in this suite that was made for romance.

What was he up to? Because with Cal there was always a plan.

She followed him into the living area and then across the hall and into another bedroom. He was already starting to strip. His jacket was strewn on the end of the bed and he was working on his tie.

"Hey, darlin'. Need help with the zipper on your dress?"

She did, but that wasn't why she'd come in.

"Spin around," he told her. When she didn't

comply, he took her shoulders and turned her himself. "It's got one of those hook thingies. Hang on. These always stump me."

He shoved his hand into the back of her dress, probably farther than was necessary to unhook a simple hook-and-eye closure. It took him a long damn time to work it. All the while he stroked her skin and moved her closer and closer to him. She was pretty sure she was too close now for him to have any kind of angle at all to work the hook. She slid back another half step and came right up against him. Then she heard the rasp of the zipper and felt a rush of cool air on her skin. He brought the zipper all the way down past her waist.

His touch was featherlight on her exposed skin, scattering goose bumps. Her chest heaved with the effort to breathe, and she was caught between wanting him to rip her dress away and fear that he actually might do it and leave her with a choice to make.

Then his fingers were gone. "There you go." He gave her a perfunctory pat on the shoulder. "Go get changed into something comfortable. I have plans for us after we eat." He disappeared into the adjoining bathroom and closed the door. A second later she heard the shower.

She shivered, more turned on than she'd been in a long time, and actually contemplated following him into the bathroom. Instead she fled to the safety of her room.

~

CAL PUT a hand on the tiled wall and jerked faster on his dick. He hadn't masturbated this much since he was fifteen and had accidentally come across a nudie magazine in his father's garage. He thought of Lucy and the way her breasts had nearly tumbled out of the top of her dress when he'd unzipped it. He imagined gripping the front and ripping it down to her waist and then lifting the back of her dress and pounding into her from behind.

He came with a jerk and a long, low groan. It wasn't enough. Goddammit, he wanted her. He wanted her in a way he hadn't wanted anything or anyone ever. She was his wife but not *his*. He was going to have to earn her back, earn her trust, earn her love. He'd do it if it killed him and he grew calluses from jerking off nearly every hour of every day. She'd be his and they could do option number thirty a hundred times a day until they passed out from exhaustion.

He shut the water off and grabbed a towel. He knew she expected him to make a move on her. It was their wedding night. What else did newly married couples do except fuck like they'd never get to fuck again. And goddammit he was hard all over again. He looked down at himself and laughed. This would be part of his penance—having a perpetual hard-on. He'd survived worse, he supposed...but not much. Being around Lucy and unable able to touch her, make her sigh and scream his name was a crueler punishment than any he could've ever come up with.

He dressed in loose sweats and a T-shirt. Just about the least sexy thing he could come up with. This was about Lucy and helping her feel safe and secure. It was about trust and commitment, two words he hadn't ever given much thought to before he'd seen the photos of Lucy and the way her eyes went blank when she thought he was going to make a move on her.

He wanted to punch something so badly. That son-of-a-bitch ex of hers had taken the most precious, most vital woman Cal had ever met and made her a shell filled with fear and shame. Cal would bring her back. She was already starting to come back to him in tiny increments. He'd go slow with her if it killed him. And it just might.

There was a knock on the door. Cal went out into the living area. The double doors to Lucy's bedroom were closed, but he could hear the water of a shower running. He opened the door to room service and signed the check as they set everything up. Lucy wouldn't be expecting what he had planned for them.

He poured himself a glass of wine and stood at the window overlooking the city, waiting for his wife. His wife. The moment he'd slipped his ring on her finger and pledged himself to her, he'd known he could never go back. He could never look at another woman and not compare her to Lucy.

He heard the door behind him open, but he didn't turn.

"Oh," she exclaimed. "Dinner. I'm starving."

He turned then and nearly wished he hadn't. She was wearing a robe, her hair wrapped in a towel on top of her head. Her skin was scrubbed pink and clean. The scent of whatever soap or shampoo she'd used coasted toward him, stroking him like a lover. She wore nothing beneath the robe, and it nearly brought him to his knees. God couldn't be this cruel to him. Surely he hadn't been that wicked.

She sashayed toward the table and plopped herself down. The rest of his wine disappeared in two desperate gulps.

"Wait," he said as she reached for one of the lids. "We're going to play a game."

She tilted her head to the side. "With food?"

"Sure. Why not make dinner fun?"

She looked like she might argue and then she withdrew her hand, relenting to him. "Okay. What are the rules?"

"The rules are we're both blindfolded."

"Why?"

"No utensils," he continued without answering. "I feed you, you feed me, and we have to guess what we're eating."

"But you ordered everything. You already know what's here."

"No. Actually I don't. I asked the kitchen to prepare a variety of finger foods, but I didn't specify what they would be. We'll both be surprised."

"Can't we just eat? I'm starving."

"You'll eat what I feed you. It'll be fun. Now close your eyes. Please."

"You first."

"Okay." He sat next to her at the table and rolled two napkins. He handed one to her. "Put this around my eyes and then put this other one around yours." He waited as she tied the napkin around his head, cutting off all sight. After a few moments he asked, "Is your blindfold on?"

"Yes."

"Okay. You go first. Lift a lid and then feed me what's underneath."

He waited, listening as she fumbled over the metal covers, and then he heard one hit the floor.

"I didn't know what to do with it," she explained.

He grinned. She was getting into this game. "We'll pick it up later. Don't worry about it."

Her hand hit him mid chest and then climbed slowly toward his throat and chin. She put her palm on his cheek, and her thumb swept across his lips. He opened his mouth, and she pushed something rough coated into it. He moved it around and then bit into it.

"Chicken nuggets," he guessed.

"I have no idea. I can't see anything."

"Okay. My turn."

He felt around on the table until his hand hit one of the plates, then he moved his hand to the next one, then the next and lifted the cover. Whatever it was, it was kind of slimy. Shrimp maybe?

Reaching across with his other hand, he found her knee and grazed the outside of her thigh, over her hip and arm, across her shoulder to her neck, and up her throat to her lips, which were parted in apprehension or expectation, he wasn't sure. Sliding his thumb along the seam, he parted them farther and slipped the bite into her mouth.

He kept his hand on her jaw as she chewed then swallowed.

"Mmm, shrimp. My turn."

He wished he could see her and her reactions. The soft sighs and throaty moans she made when he fed her something she liked drove him nuts. They were the same sounds she made during sex. Three bites later, he ripped his blindfold off to find Lucy watching him.

"You cheated," he declared.

She laughed, tipping her head back. "I just took my blindfold off. I swear. And shut up. You cheated too."

"I can't help it. I'm starving." He placed both his hands on her knees and leaned in. "Feed me."

She stared at him for a moment and then reached out without seeing where her hand landed and grabbed something. "Here." She pressed a mini quiche into his mouth, filling it, and watched as he chewed and swallowed.

"My turn." He picked up a strawberry that was almost too large for her and slipped it partway through her lips. "Bite."

He bit into the other half of the strawberry and their lips touched briefly before he pulled away.

Lucy couldn't believe what they were doing. This had to be the most erotic thing she'd ever done. They took turns feeding each other until she was so full she thought she'd burst.

"That was fun, but I can't eat another bite," she told him. "Is there any more wine left?"

He lifted the bottle and poured the last bit into her glass, then tipped it upside down in the bucket. Settling back into his chair, he took a sip of his wine. A comfortable silence settled over them as they gazed out at the view of the Dallas skyline.

He was the first to break it. "Can I ask you a question?"

"Sure."

"What do you want to do?"

"Tonight?"

"No, with yourself. Have you ever thought about going back to school and finishing your degree?"

She couldn't believe he remembered her talking about doing just that when they'd been together the first time. Quitting school was one of the things she regretted most in her life besides her marriage to Kevin. Since then she'd hardly been able to think past next week let alone a year or more from now. "I used to."

"You could do it. Go back to school I mean. You've got Sam to watch over Poppy now and no job. The corporate things I'd need you for would mainly occur in the evenings. You have days free to take classes if you want to."

"I guess I hadn't thought it would be an option, so I haven't given it any consideration."

"What kinds of classes would you take? What are you interested in?"

"You ask really tough questions."

He shrugged a shoulder. "Not that tough. What did you want to be when you grew up?"

"Well, when I was four, I wanted to be a ballerina. You've seen my dancing skills, so that would've been a bust. Then when I was twelve I was crazy about horses, but I don't think you could make a living at that. I went through a series of occupations—veterinarian, singer of a rock band, interior designer, firefighter—"

"Firefighter?"

"I was dating a guy who had just started at the academy so..." She shrugged. "I did look into nursing a couple of months ago, but I didn't have the funds for school, so that was out."

"You have the funds now."

"No, you have the funds."

"Lucy, we're married. What's mine is yours."

"That's a fair trade for me, but not for you. Besides nursing school would take longer than our marriage would last, and then what?"

He looked down at his hands folded in his lap. "Yup. One year. That was the deal."

"I think I'm ready for the Jacuzzi now." She stood up and adjusted her robe.

He grabbed the belt of her robe. "This year can be anything we want it to be. Anything at all." He tugged, making her move toward him. "Sign up for that school if that's what you want, darlin'. If you like, you can think of it as my parting gift to you. I won't be the reason you don't follow your dreams. I won't hold you down or hold you back. Ever."

"You don't have to—"

"I know I don't." His voice held a quiet sort of anger. He jerked on her tie again, and she had to grab it with both hands to keep her robe from popping open. "I want to. Let me."

"Cal." Lucy searched his face for some kind of clue

as to what was going to happen next. Knowing what was coming had saved her more than a time or two when things got angry and out of control.

"Do you think just once you could let me give you something without questioning my motives?"

She gripped her robe tighter, the familiar spiral where everything suddenly turned against her reaching out for her. "I'll do whatever you want, Cal."

"Whatever I want?"

She nodded.

"Sit down."

She made to go back to her chair, but he still had a hold of her.

"On my lap." He patted his leg with his free hand.

She watched him, wondering what he was playing at. He'd become all serious and calm as though he was asking her to do something simple or this was some kind of test. He made no move other than the smile that crept slowly across his face.

"Sit down, darlin'."

She lowered herself onto his leg, balancing so she could pop up at any moment.

"Now, put your head right here." He patted his shoulder.

"Why?"

"You said you'd do whatever I wanted. I want to hold you, darlin'."

She lowered her gaze to his shoulder and then felt herself leaning in. His arms came up around her, loose and comforting. It had been a long time since a man had held her. She settled against him, placing her hands on his chest. This was a dangerous proposition. This hope that unfurled slowly, uncertainly.

She trusted him, she suddenly realized. And that was the most dangerous thing she could ever do. Because if she trusted him, she'd let him in. Once he got in, she didn't think she could ever get him back out.

8

She tucked herself in tight, bringing her legs up and curling into him like a child. Cal held her tighter, dropping his cheek to the top of her head. She was so warm and good smelling. And soft, so soft. Her skin, her hair, her lush curves pressed against him. He inhaled, taking more of her in as though he needed her very essence to survive.

He was an idiot to think that he could ever let her go again.

"Cal?"

"Hmm?"

"Thank you."

"What for?"

"The wedding was really beautiful. And my dress... I've never worn one like it. And the flowers and the decorations... It was all perfect."

"I'm glad you liked it since you picked everything out."

She nudged his shoulder. "You know what I mean. None of it was necessary."

"Darlin', it was all necessary. And worth it."

"It wasn't, but thank you for it anyway."

"You're welcome."

She yawned. "I think I'm too tired for the Jacuzzi."

"Me too. Seems a shame not to use it though. Maybe tomorrow before we leave."

"This is the first time I've ever been away from Poppy. I'm not sure how much longer I can bear to stay away from her."

Running a hand over her hair, he chuckled. "Well then, we'll just have to come back some other time."

Her little hand snaked up and around his neck to play with his hair as he was doing with hers. "Seems kind of extravagant."

"But fun."

"Yeah."

She snuggled deeper into him, and her other hand came around his waist to his back. She was getting bolder. He could sit like this with her forever.

"Cal?"

"Yes, darlin'?"

"Could I...?" She let out a breath that blew hot against his neck. "Could I ask you a favor?"

"Sure."

"Stop sneaking Poppy that sugary cereal. I can't get her to eat the good stuff anymore."

He pulled back to look at her. "How did you know?"

"I can smell it on her, and the other day her cheek was still sticky from it. It's not good for her."

"I was bribing her to like me, but I'll stop."

"You don't need to bribe her to like you. She likes you almost better than she likes me."

"Then the bribes worked. What can I bribe *you* with?" He was close enough to kiss her. All he had to do was lean down a bit.

"You don't need to bribe me either."

"You mean you already like me?"

"Maybe more than I should."

His gaze dropped to her mouth. "How much do you like me?"

"Definitely more than I should."

"Enough to let me kiss you?"

"Yeah," she whispered. "Just enough."

He lowered his mouth to hers. Her hand at his nape encouraged him to get closer. Then they were kissing. A light, testing kind of kiss as though they were learning each other all over again. And maybe they were. They definitely weren't the same people they'd been seventeen months ago. He kept it easy, enjoying the feel of her at this new angle and the way she sifted her hand through his hair. Everything felt new and a little scary. A fragile kind of peace was building between them. He'd have to step lightly, careful not to trample it the way he'd so carelessly done before.

Reluctantly breaking the kiss, he glanced down at her to gage her reaction. Her lids stayed closed a moment and then she sighed.

"You're really good at that," she whispered, her eyes fluttering open.

Her compliment made him grin. She always kept him a tad off balance.

"So are you," he answered back.

"We should do that more often."

"I agree. We can do it as often as you'd like."

"I think I should go to bed now."

"All right."

She disentangled herself from him, stood, and adjusted her robe. Tucking her arms around herself tight, she looked at him as though he was an unsolvable puzzle. "I'm not sure what to believe here."

"What do you want to believe?"

"I don't know."

"I think you do, but you're too afraid."

"I'm not afraid."

"Then what are you?"

"Cautious. If it was just me..."

"If it was just you, what? What would you do?" he challenged.

She shifted her stance, flipping her hair over her shoulder. "I'd ask you to come to bed with me."

"But you won't because of Poppy."

"If I'm wrong—"

"You're not wrong, and you're not asking me to go to bed with you because you're afraid."

"I am not."

"What are you scared of? What's going to happen if we sleep together?"

"I might start believing in you again."

"You're already starting to believe in me or else you wouldn't have brought up taking me to your bed."

"Never mind. Forget I said anything."

She turned to go, but he grabbed her arm. Trying to pull out of his grip, she shrank from him, a desperate, wide-eyed look on her face.

"Lucy, stop. Settle down."

"Let go of me."

"Okay."

He released her, and she stepped out of his reach, staring at him as though she was trying to anticipate what he might do next.

"When I reach for you—" he began in the gentlest tone he could manage with the rage he felt against her ex boiling just below the surface. If he ever got a hold of that asshole... "—it will be to stroke you, to soothe you, or to get you so hot for me you can't think of anything but having me buried deep inside you. It will never be to hurt you."

"I don't know what you're talking about."

"I've hurt you in a lot of ways, Lucy. I know that. I have to live with it and find a way to make up for it. But I will never harm you physically. Ever."

"I know you won't."

"Good." But she didn't, not really. It was more about her wanting to believe than the actual believing of it. But it was a start, a place for them to begin. "I swear to you, darlin', that I will do everything in my power to never hurt you again. And I want more than anything to accept your non-offer to take you to bed. You don't know how much I want that. But I won't. Not until we get some things settled between us that only time and new experiences can create."

"What kind of new experiences?" He could tell she was curious. And interested.

"The kind that make you forget and forgive. I'm going to earn your forgiveness if it's the last thing I do. And then you'll forget why you were mad at me in the first place."

"And how are you going to do that?"

"I'm going to woo you."

"Woo me. That's backward, isn't it? Seeing as how we're already married."

"I still have my work cut out for me though, don't I?"

She pressed her lips together. "Hmm."

"I'm up for the challenge."

"Why? I thought this was just a business arrangement. You're paying me to be your wife, for crying out loud. That's not exactly romantic."

"The idea was that I would help you and you would help me. Except you haven't cashed your check. Technically no money has changed hands. By the way, why haven't you cashed it?"

"I don't know."

"Maybe you see the same potential here that I do. Maybe you remember how good it used to be between us. Maybe you want me in your bed so bad it's all you can think about."

"And maybe it would be a moot point anyway because your head would be too big to fit through my bedroom door."

Lucy was pretty sure this man had gone insane, and then he threw his head back and laughed and she *knew* he had. He certainly wasn't the same Cal she'd been with before. That Cal would've had her robe open and her begging for release within three minutes of her walking into the room. *This* Cal held her gently and asked to kiss her and woo her. She wasn't quite sure what to do with this Cal. The only thing she knew for sure was that she wanted to take him to bed and find out all of the other ways in which he'd changed.

"You are definitely right about that, darlin'. And that's what got me into hot water with you in the first place. But I'm here now, willing to try. What do you say, will you be my girl?"

"Are you asking your wife to go steady with you? You have gone crazy."

"Crazy about you. Come here and kiss me good night."

He slid his hand down her arm and tugged on her wrist. This time she didn't resist him. He brought her to stand between his legs. She put her hands on his shoulders and looked down into the wildest blue eyes she'd ever seen. She was crazy about him too, but it wasn't the same as it had been before. Back then she'd been crazy blind with need for him and just plain all around crazy blind where he was concerned. She wondered if maybe he was more dangerous to her now than he'd ever been before.

He put his hands at her waist, then smoothed them up her back. "Give me a kiss good night." His voice held all the wicked promise of the old Cal, but his words were the gentle promise and boast of the new Cal.

She leaned down and gave him a chaste good-night kiss. He didn't pressure her for more and let her slip away from him toward her bedroom.

"Good night."

"Good night, darlin'."

9

It had been two weeks since her husband had asked her to go steady with him and had started to court her. They'd been on seven dates, and he'd come to the door with flowers each time. At the end of the night he'd escorted her to her bedroom door, kissed her good night and then walked across the hall to his room. It was very strange and kind of thrilling.

It also made it hard to keep her mind on planning her first dinner party as Mrs. Cal Sellers. The caterer had already had to break her out of her daydreaming twice during their meeting, and even now Lucy struggled to follow what he was saying. Something about aperitifs and amuse-bouches, whatever they were. She nodded along, trusting that this man knew more about fancy dinner parties than she did. After all, it was his job.

"Mrs. Sellers?"

Lucy looked up to find their housekeeper in the dining room doorway. "Yes, Hazel?"

"There's a delivery at the gate. Were you expecting it?"

"What kind of delivery?"

"Flowers. For you."

"Oh. No, I wasn't expecting it."

"From your husband?" The caterer winked.

"Probably. The flowers for the party aren't supposed to arrive until day after tomorrow, right?"

"Correct."

"Should I let them up?" Hazel asked.

"Yes, please. Thank you, Hazel."

"Now about the table décor," the caterer went on. "I think a long, low centerpiece would set things off nicely. Here's a photo of what I had in mind." He handed her his tablet to look at.

"Oh, that's pretty. Yes, that one."

"Excellent. Then we're all done here."

He packed up his things, and she showed him to the door, uncertain of everything she'd chosen. She wanted the party to be perfect and for Cal to be proud of her. He'd more than held up his end of their bargain, and now she was going to play hostess to the man whose company Cal wanted to buy. The company that could mean millions to Sellers Investments.

As the caterer went out the door, the deliveryman came up the walk carrying the largest bouquet of roses Lucy had ever seen. It was a wonder the man could see where he was going. Cal had outdone himself this time.

"Sign here." He thrust a clipboard at her.

She started to sign her name, except it was the

wrong name on the order form. "There must be a mistake. My last name's not Walker, it's Sellers."

The deliveryman thrust the flowers off to the side and grabbed for her, pulling her through the doorway. He put a hand to her throat and pinned her up against the house. "Your name will always be Mrs. Kevin Walker no matter who you spread your legs for."

The shock of seeing Kevin was eclipsed only by the sheer terror of his fingers digging into her windpipe. She couldn't move, thrust back to the days when she lived under his brutal hands and the pain he could inflict.

His grip tightened on her throat as he lifted her. "You're a whore."

She fought for air, her hands coming up to pry at his, her legs scrambling for purchase. He shoved a hand between her legs and squeezed. Spots danced in front of her eyes. She reached out blindly, trying to get at him, and caught him in the face, raking his cheek with her nails. He howled in pain and released her. She slid down the side of the house.

"Bitch!" He smacked her face hard, knocking her flat.

She curled into a ball as he drew his foot back to kick her. Only the blow never landed. A grunt and sickening, bone-crunching sound brought her head up. Sam the nanny stood over Kevin, who writhed on the ground, covering his face with his hands, blood gushing from between his fingers.

"Are you all right, Mrs. Sellers?" Sam asked, keeping his gaze on Kevin.

Lucy put her hand over her stinging cheek. "Yeah. I think so."

"I don't care who you fuck," Kevin said, his voice muffled by his hands. "I want my daughter back."

"She's not yours." She staggered to her feet, the rage against her ex rising inside her. "She's mine. And you're not getting anything but the hell out of here."

"I'm calling the police," Sam said.

Kevin struggled to stand. "You're nothing but a bitch and a whore. I'm going to get my daughter back if I have to kill you to do it."

Lucy got as close to him as she dared. "You'll never get her. I'll kill you before you ever lay a hand on her."

He lunged for her, but Sam leapt, swinging his leg up and connecting with Kevin's jaw. Kevin folded and dropped to the grass, unconscious. Lucy glanced from Sam to Kevin then back again.

"Where'd you learn that?"

"Nanny school."

"You did not learn that in nanny school."

Sam shrugged, then bent to turn Kevin on his stomach and secured his hands with a zip tie. Not exactly normal nanny paraphernalia. Kevin was still out when Sam rolled him onto his back again and checked his pulse.

Sam looked up at Lucy. "You should get some ice on that cheek. It's starting to swell. And you've got a little blood right here." He motioned toward the corner of his mouth.

She wiped at the blood and put her palm to her hot cheek. It would probably bruise too. How was she going to explain this to Cal's business associates two nights from now? How was she going to explain this to Cal?

"We've got a little situation here," Sam said into his phone. "I've got it handled, but you may want to see about your wife."

Lucy waved her hands at Sam. "Don't tell him," she whispered. "I'm okay."

Kevin had invaded their home. The police had been summoned. This was not part of their bargain. Their arrangement might have started out as a business deal, but it was starting to become more than that. The last thing she wanted was for her past with Kevin to invade her present with Cal.

"Her ex showed up at the house," Sam said into his phone. "By the time I heard what was going on he had her on the ground."

Lucy glared at Sam as best she could with one partially swollen eye.

"He got her in the face before I could stop him. He's out cold and cuffed right now. The police are on their way." He held his phone away from his ear. She could plainly hear Cal's string of expletives from where she stood. When there was a pause, Sam put the phone back to his ear. "No, sir. But she could use some ice, and she'll probably have a shiner." He held the phone out again. "Yes, sir. I understand. I'll give you a full report when you get here." He hung up. "You should get that ice," he said to Lucy.

"You're not really a nanny, are you?"

"Yes, ma'am, I am."

"Then you're not *just* a nanny. What else are you?"

"British Special Forces. Formerly." He pointed to his cheek. "If you don't get that ice, I've been instructed to call you an ambulance. A bag of frozen peas works well."

Sirens wailed in the distance.

"Fine."

She stormed into the house and grabbed the next best thing—a bag of frozen corn wrapped in a towel. On her way back outside she caught sight of herself in the mirror in the entryway. Kevin sure knew how to cause the most damage from the least amount of effort. But then he'd had a lot of practice. She put some spit on her finger and wiped at the blood at the corner of her mouth. She was going to be bruised from her jaw to her eye. His ring had caught her mouth and split the skin, but it wasn't as bad as it could've been. Thank God Sam had been there to stop it.

By the time she got back to where Sam stood over a just-coming-around Kevin, the police were rolling up. They took her and Sam's statements and put Kevin in the back of one of the cruisers.

She was finishing up with one of the officers when Cal arrived. He took one look at her and stalled. His face went pale. She had the makeshift ice pack over the worst of it. Wait until he saw what was underneath.

"That's my husband," she told the officer when they stopped him at the edge of the walk. "Please let him through."

Cal approached her slowly, his gaze never leaving her. He looked...heartbroken. There was no other way to describe it. She'd never seen that expression on him.

Tears pinched the backs of her eyes. He gently drew the ice pack down.

"Oh, darlin'," he breathed.

That was all it took. She burst into tears. He wrapped her in his arms.

"I'm sorry," he kept repeating. "I'm so sorry."

She gripped the back of his jacket and held on. This was all her fault. She'd brought this to his home—the police, the drama. It would probably make the news. Not exactly the kind of family values Cal wanted to present.

She pulled back to look up at him. "No. I'm sorry. I brought all of this to you, to your home—"

"Shh. This isn't your fault. I knew what he was capable of, and I didn't adequately protect you."

"What do you mean you knew?"

"Mrs. Sellers," one of the officers interrupted. "Here's my card with the case number." He handed her a card. "If you have any questions, give us a call."

Cal glanced up past the officer and spotted her asshole ex in the back of one of the police cars. Before he thought to do it, he was moving in that direction. He'd never wanted to hurt someone so bad in all his life. He came right up to the car window and banged on it with the side of his fist. He wanted this asshole's full attention.

"You ever touch my wife or come within a thousand feet of her again and I will end you."

"Sir. Back away from the car," one of the officers warned.

"Cal, don't," Lucy pleaded, pulling on his arm. "He's not worth it."

Cal stepped away.

"She's a whore," Kevin yelled. "She's always been nothing but a whore."

Cal went for him but was held back by Sam and one of the officers. "I mean it," Cal shouted. "Stay away from her." He jerked out of their grasp. Wrapping an arm around Lucy, he eased her up the walk and into the house.

He brought her into his office and closed the door behind them. Leaning back against it, he tipped his head up and closed his eyes. The bastard got to her. It was all he could think about the whole way home and then when he saw her and the damage to her face... Son of a bitch! He had one job, *one*—to protect her— and he'd fucked it up.

"I'm sorry." He opened his eyes to look at her.

"It's my fault. I wasn't paying attention... I never dreamed he'd come here. I'm so, so sorry. I should've told you about him. This wasn't part of the bargain, all this chaos and the publicity... Oh, Cal, I'm so sorry. Your dinner party... I've ruined everything." She burst into tears again, and it was like someone twisted a knife in his chest.

He went to her and held her. "No, darlin'. This is my fault, not yours."

She looked up at him with her watery eyes and half-swollen face, and he wanted to punch something. "What did you mean outside when you said that you knew what he was capable of? I never told you anything about him. In fact, now that I think about it, you've never asked about him or my time with him."

"Why in the hell would I want to hear about you and another man?"

She pulled away from him and wiped at the tears still falling down her face, each one like acid on his heart.

"You're avoiding my question, and I know why. You had him investigated, didn't you?" Her expression changed from disbelief to anger. "Oh, my God. That's why you hired Sam—to protect us. I know he's not just a nanny. He's Special Forces, for God's sake. Well, let's have it." She flung her hands out, then crossed her arms over her chest. "All of it. What do you know?"

"Now, darlin'." He tried to soothe her, his mind running through what needed to be done to insure his wife and daughter's safety. "This isn't the time to hash this out. I need to get Lucas on the line so he can get his guys down here to rework our security."

He'd hire four, no six guards around the clock, with a new security procedure for anyone trying to get through the front gate. Walker had gotten past it too easily. If he could, then anyone could. He'd promised her they'd be safe here. They weren't. None of them were. He moved toward his desk to make a list of everything they were going to need.

"Cal Sellers, you stop avoiding my question and answer me right now!"

He pulled up short and turned toward her. "Fine. You really want to know? Hell yes, I had him investigated. You were a cagey little thing when it came to answering questions about him. I asked you flat out why he didn't have visitation with Poppy, and while you didn't lie, you didn't exactly tell the truth, did you? Otherwise you would've told me about the restraining order and the multiple, *multiple* arrests for beating you bloody."

He stalked toward her, angry with her and her asshole ex, but mostly he was furious with himself. "I saw the pictures of you, Lucy. I *saw* them. So, yeah. I knew what I was getting into with you when I married you and I did it anyway."

Lucy couldn't believe it. She was such an idiot. Cal hadn't married her because he'd wanted her. He'd married her as some kind of community service penance. She'd carried the shame of what she'd been through for months and months, hiding the worst of it from everyone in her life including Lucas and Mi, and now because of Cal's need to know and control *everything*, her life had been broken open for everyone to inspect and judge. They'd look at her with pity in their eyes, and she'd always be a victim. She'd always be the woman who stupidly stayed with a man who beat her.

"You married me *anyway*?" She struggled to keep her emotions in check. "How good of you. You must have been pretty damn desperate to stoop so low. And sneaky too, going behind my back and getting Lucas to investigate me."

"Sneaky? Look who's talking? You've been hiding a hell of a lot from me, haven't you? You can't blame me for going out and getting answers on my own."

Her worst fears confirmed. They knew. They'd seen

the photos of her at her very lowest. The degradation. How desperate and sad she must seem to them all now.

She fought back against the rising tide of humiliation the only way she knew how. "Did you ever think that I *have* to hide things from you because I never know when I'm going to walk in on you screwing your secretary?"

"Now we're getting down to it, aren't we? You still don't trust me or believe me when I tell you that I didn't screw her."

"Wanting to screw her and actually screwing her are *the same thing* in this case. If I hadn't walked in on you and stopped you, you would've *actually* screwed her. So why should I trust you when you'd throw everything away in an instant for a ride up a short skirt?"

"I've been here every day trying in every way I know how to show you that you can trust me. I'm not the same selfish asshole I was back then."

"Oh, yeah? If you're trying to earn back my trust, then why didn't you wait and ask me again later about Kevin instead of going behind my back? From where I'm standing, the new improved Cal looks and acts a lot like the old Cal."

He let out a breath, his shoulders sagging. "You're right. I might not have had sex with her, but that doesn't mean I wasn't working my way around to it. I was an asshole to do that to you. I ruined everything between us. It's my fault you ran off and married a man who abused you. And now here we are back together, and you're still getting hurt because of me."

She stared at him, trying to work out what to do

with him. The old Cal would've never acknowledged his mistakes and failings. Maybe he had changed. Him acknowledging his part in what had happened between them forced her to look at what was happening between them now. He was right. She should've confided in him from the beginning of this whole thing. He'd offered her a way out, knowing that she came to him with more baggage than a commercial airliner. He'd made a bad bargain when he'd married her, but like he said, he'd known it from the start and had married her anyway. There had to be something recoverable in that.

"Huh." A corner of her mouth tugged up at the irony. "We're a messed-up pair, aren't we?"

Cal nearly dropped to his knees in relief. He hadn't totally screwed things up. She was offering him forgiveness or at the very least understanding. He grasped at it, afraid it would suddenly slip away. "Yes we are, darlin'. Yes we are."

"I'm going to get this out here and now because I don't know where any of this is going. You've made me feel special and cherished with your flowers and dates and kisses good night. I'm starting to believe in you, Cal Sellers, and it scares the hell out of me.

"I couldn't take it if I walked in on you with another woman again. I don't know what I'd do, but I know I couldn't take it. You darn near destroyed me last time, and I ran to the first person who showed me any kindness. Out of the frying pan and into the fire. It was my choice to marry Kevin. I own my part in that. I'm trying really hard to trust you. I want to trust you, but you can't go off all half-cocked behind my back. If you want to know something about me, then you ask me."

"And you'll tell me the truth? No hedging or skating around or leaving out the parts you don't want to talk about?"

She hesitated, then nodded. "Yes."

"All right then. I won't go snooping around where I don't belong. Come here." He held out his hand to her, and she took it. "I'm going to say this to *you* right here right now. I take my marriage vows to you very seriously. There isn't a woman alive who could tempt me away from you.

"I know I've hurt you, and I paid the price for it when I lost you and had to stand in the back of that church, watching you pledge your heart and body to someone else. I swore if I ever got a chance with you again I'd be the kind of man you deserved and who deserved you."

He put a hand on her good cheek. "I want to kiss you so bad."

She leaned into him, pressing her body right up against his. He got so hard thinking about laying her down on the couch and showing her how much he wanted her and this second chance with her. But he didn't. Instead he waited, like a virgin kissing a girl for the first time, for her to give him permission. It was a humbling thing to have to ask his wife for a kiss and be unsure of her answer.

10

Lucy went up on her toes and brushed her lips across Cal's. He cupped her face so he wouldn't be tempted to let his hands wander over her. He wasn't kidding when he'd told her he liked the way she looked now—all womanly curves and large, full breasts. And her ass. My God, her ass. He wanted to grip it in both hands, haul her up against his erection, and show her what she did to him with nothing more than her body pressed to his and his lips on hers.

He broke the kiss and glanced down at his wife. She was so beautiful even with the swelling and the bruising that she took his breath away. "You're a gift I don't deserve. I promise to do my damnedest to make you happy. I want you. And if you ever decide you want me, I promise to make you glad you married me. As many times and in as many ways as you'd like."

"I don't doubt that since you've already proven yourself in that arena."

He grinned like the sinner he was. "And yet I still feel like I have something to prove with you. One of these days, darlin', one of these days, I'll make good on my promise, and when I do, you'll have made me the happiest man alive." He turned her face to examine the bruise just beginning to darken under her eye. "You need more ice. And a hot bath." He leaned in and placed a gentle kiss on her cheek. "I could kill him for laying a hand on you."

"Don't. He's not worth it."

"Did he ever hurt Poppy?"

"No. She almost never came to his notice except when he wanted to brag about her or use her to get me to do what he wanted."

He brought her hand up to his lips and kissed it. "Go up and take your bath. I'll look in on her. I need to make sure she's safe."

"Sam's with her, so I'm sure she is. But I know what you mean. I think I'll go up with you."

They walked side by side up the stairs, holding hands. He felt both excited and nervous around her as if he were on the verge of completing a huge merger that would make him richer than any man had the right to be. He risked a sideways glance at her. How could he have ever looked at another woman, let alone touched her? He'd been the biggest, most arrogant fool to walk the earth back then. He'd learned his lesson. He would do better by her. He was certainly willing to give it his all.

They found Poppy in the playroom with Sam, who was reading her a book. When they walked in, Poppy clapped her hands and broke out into a huge grin. For Cal. The air in his chest expanded, making it hard for him to breathe. She filled places inside him he hadn't known were empty. She was *his*.

"There's my girl." Lucy rushed over and scooped up her baby, showering her with kisses.

Sam got up from the chair and came over to Cal. "I'm sorry I arrived too late," he whispered. "By the time I got there he'd hit her in the face and was about to kick her."

"You stopped him."

"Yes, sir."

"Then you got there in time. I can't thank you enough, Sam, for saving my Lucy. I don't know what I'd do if anything happened to her or Poppy."

"I'll be giving a full account of what happened today to Mr. Vega."

"Could you include your security recommendations? I have some ideas of how we can tighten up, but you're more of an expert than me. I'd appreciate your suggestions."

"Yes, sir."

"Thank you. Why don't you go on downstairs and relax for a bit. You've earned it."

Cal was alone with his girls. He'd watched Lucy be a mother to their daughter many times over the past few weeks, but there was something about watching her now that made him imagine more babies with her. Another two or three, boys, girls, it didn't matter, as long as they greeted him the way Poppy did now, trying to leap out of her mother's arms toward him.

"Come here, sweet pea." He scooped her out of Lucy's arms and held her. "Did you miss me?"

"She could care less who I am when you're around."

"I believe your momma's jealous. Another female's captured my heart, and she just can't take it, can she?"

Poppy grabbed his cheeks so she could rub noses with him. It had become their thing.

"I'm the bringer of food and baths. You're the big giant plaything who sneaks her sugary cereal—don't think I don't know you still do that—and who gives her horsey rides and tickles her."

"Well, darlin', I can't help it if she likes me better."

"It's all that bribing."

"You do what works for you and I'll do what works for me. Why don't you go take that bath, and I'll keep working my wiles on Miss Poppy."

Lucy hesitated. Watching Poppy with Cal worried her. The more attached she got to him the harder it would be if she had to leave.

"All right. I won't be long," she said.

"We'll be fine. Go on." He picked up a book, sat down in the rocker with Poppy, and started reading to her.

As Lucy ran the water in the tub, she couldn't get the sight of Cal holding Poppy out of her head. It made her long for things that might never be. Poppy deserved a father who loved her and who would be there for her. In that regard she'd failed her daughter, she thought as she lowered into the steaming bath water. The first father she'd given her daughter had been neglectful when he hadn't been abusive and cruel. And now here was Cal wanting to fill the role that should've been his in the first place.

But Lucy still wasn't convinced that Cal had made a full one-eighty where women were concerned. She hadn't been joking when she'd told him his cheating a second time would destroy her. She'd been more than halfway to falling in love with Cal when she'd walked into his office that fateful afternoon and caught him between the legs of his secretary, her skirt hiked up, his tongue in her mouth, and his hand up her blouse.

She'd stumbled out of his office and down the hall with Cal on her heels. He'd finally caught up to her in the elevator, stammering excuses and mumbling half-hearted apologies. She hadn't believed a word he'd said then, but now...now she was starting to believe, and that was the most dangerous thing she could ever do.

Because if she believed him, she'd start to trust him. If she trusted him, she'd have to tell him the truth about what happened after she walked out of his office that day. And once it was out, there would be no going back.

With thoughts of Cal and Poppy tumbling around in her head, she couldn't get comfortable in the tub, so she climbed out and toweled off. It had only been a couple weeks since she and Cal had started spending time together again in this weird married-but-not-quite-a-couple gray area.

She'd watch him when he wasn't paying attention and she'd remember the good times and what it had felt like to have all of Cal's attention. What it had felt like to have his hands on her...and his mouth, his

incredibly talented, seductive mouth. He'd seduced her
with words and then put all of it into action, backing up
his boasts with skill.

The first time they'd slept together had been an
accident. They'd been at a launch party for one of the
products that would be featured on *Pleasure at Home*.
She'd been with the show for a couple of years by then.
When she bumped into him at the bar and he offered
to buy her a free drink with a wink, she accepted. He
was cute, and even though he was her boss's boss and
therefore off limits, she didn't hide her interest in him.
A couple hours later and they were slipping out the
back door and climbing into his Porsche. He took her to
his place. Probably to impress her. It had.

Before she knew it they'd been on the stairs to the
second floor, ripping each other's clothes off. They'd
made it as far as the landing and then he was on top of
her, sliding into her, her legs wrapped around his waist.
She'd never come so hard, so fast in all her life. Then
he'd taken her back downstairs and fixed her an
omelet. They'd done it a second time with her bent
over the countertop and him driving into her from
behind.

She hadn't gotten to see his bedroom until two
weeks later. By that time they'd had sex on every available horizontal surface and even a few not so horizontal. It had gone on like that between them for months.
He could hardly keep his hands off her. When she'd
walked in on him with someone else, she'd been
beyond shocked and humiliated. It had brought her

world down around her. And then she'd met Kevin. He'd been everything Cal hadn't. Or so she'd thought.

Lucy changed into clean clothes and went down the hall to check on her husband and daughter. She found Cal rocking a sleeping Poppy. He hummed softly. She started to go into the room, but Cal's whispered words stopped her.

"If you were mine, I'd never let you go. If you were mine, I'd make sure you knew how much you were loved and wanted every day." He kissed Poppy's forehead, and Lucy's eyes filled with tears.

This was what every child should have, a father who loved her and wanted her. It was what Lucy should've had and what Poppy should've had all along. She backed out of the doorway, smothering a sob with her hand.

No matter what had happened between them, Lucy realized now that she never should've kept Poppy from her father and Cal from his daughter.

11

How was she going to tell him after all this time?

Because she had to. She had to tell him. Not only had she promised him the truth, but she couldn't sit back every day and watch him care for and cradle his daughter and not tell him the truth. When she'd initially agreed to marry him, she was only thinking of keeping Poppy safe. She hadn't expected Cal to dote so much on his daughter. How could she? He hadn't mentioned children at all in the months they'd been together. The words marriage and family had never fallen from his mouth until that afternoon when she'd come to him in an act of sheer desperation.

She'd found out she was pregnant a week after walking into the nightmare in his office. She swore then that she'd never ask Cal for anything. Ever. And she hadn't until she had to ask for her old job back.

But now things were different. Cal was different. And her feelings for him, well, they'd changed too.

Seeing him holding their daughter and wishing she was his was more than Lucy could handle. She'd tell him. Tonight.

Her mind made up, she dried her tears and took a really deep breath.

By the time she returned to Poppy's room, Cal had just put the baby in her crib and was coming back out the door.

"Nap time," he said, with a proud grin. "How're you feeling?" He examined her face. "The swelling's not as bad as it was before, but you should still keep ice on it." He ran a light finger under her eye. "It's already purple. I hate seeing his mark on you."

"I'll be okay. But what about your dinner party?"

"Already postponed. You'll have to change the date with the caterer, but that shouldn't be a problem. There's something I wanted to talk with you about, but I have to get back to the office. Will you be okay?"

"I'll be fine."

He leaned down and kissed her on her good cheek. "I'll see you tonight."

He started for the stairs, but she called him back. "Cal?"

"Yes?"

"I was thinking of maybe trying option number twelve tonight."

"Option twelve..." Cal tilted his head to the side, hardly able to believe what he was hearing. He had no idea what option twelve was, but if she wanted it, then he sure as hell would give it to her. "Oh. Is that right? And just who were you thinking of trying it with?"

"My husband. If he gets home at a decent hour."

He walked back toward her. "I'll see what I can do for you, darlin'."

"You do that."

He gave her a real kiss this time, but not the kind he had planned for her tonight. This one was easy and gentle and full of promise.

"I'll see you tonight," she promised.

He reluctantly turned away from her and headed down the stairs. As much as he wanted to stay, he had preparations to make and a mayor to call about a certain suspect that had been taken into custody today. He also had a surprise up his sleeve for Lucy, one he hoped she would agree to. There was no way he was going to allow what happened today to ever happen to her again.

He stopped to thank Sam one more time for saving Lucy, then left for his office. First order of business: call Lucas. Next order of business: look up option number twelve.

CAL SPENT the rest of the day working his tail off to get everything done that needed done so he could be home at a reasonable time. While option twelve didn't have the same flare as eleven and thirteen, it was still miles away from where he and Lucy were right now. He'd take whatever she was offering. He hoped she would be just as amenable to his suggestions.

That afternoon he'd purchased a handgun for Lucy

and arranged for shooting lessons. That way if she was ever attacked again, she would have a way to protect herself. He'd do everything in his power to make sure that asshole kept as far away from his family as possible. To that end, he'd had a long talk this afternoon with the mayor about the need to crack down on crime, especially domestic violence. If the mayor also happened to have a copy of the file Lucas had given him on Lucy's case, well, that might just light a fire under his ass.

Cal drove through the gates of home, looking forward to seeing his family. His family. Who would've thought old rabble-rousing Cal would be looking forward to getting home to his wife and daughter? Poppy had charmed him almost as much as her mother. He adored that little girl. Who could've predicted it? He'd always liked kids...in small doses. But Poppy was different. Everything she did impressed him. Maybe he'd come to that point in life where he wanted a wife and children.

The good Lord knew he was done with the bachelor life and had been for sometime. Now he had Lucy and Poppy to fill the nights he would've spent home alone. He parked his car in the garage and headed into the house. The first thing he heard was Poppy crying. Screaming actually. He dropped his briefcase and tore up the stairs.

Lucy held Poppy's stiff little body as the child reared her head back and wailed.

"What's wrong with her?" he asked, the panic in his voice making it too loud.

"Ear infection. I think. This happened once before. I called her pediatrician, but she hasn't called me back yet."

"Can't you give her anything?"

"I gave her some infant pain medication, but it hasn't kicked in yet, poor bug." Lucy rubbed the baby's back. "I know it hurts, precious." Her cell phone rang.

Cal held his hands out. "Let me have her. You answer that. And it better be that damned doctor." He took Poppy from Lucy and put her to his shoulder where she always seemed to like it best. "There now, sweet pea. I've got you. She's burning up," he told Lucy.

"Fever. I'm going to take this where it's quiet. You sure you got her?"

"We're fine. Go on."

He walked back and forth, rubbing Poppy's back and trying to soothe her. He got her quieted down to long, pitiful moans interrupted by hiccups that tore at his heart. She was so hot and sweaty that she'd soaked his dress shirt. Her red curls lay flat to her head. He kept walking with her, and she eventually fell asleep. He eased down into the recliner and closed his eyes.

Hearing her screams had scared half a year off his life. Forget the diapers and nighttime feedings. This had to be the worst part about having a child—seeing them suffer and not being able to do a damn thing about it. He didn't think he'd ever felt more helpless, except for when he'd come home and seen the damage on Lucy's beautiful face.

He settled Poppy in the crook of his arm and gently rocked her. Poor little darlin'. Tiny beads of sweat dotted her forehead and pink cheeks. He pulled a blanket through the slats of her crib, then draped it gently over her, worried she'd catch a chill from being wet.

She looked so much like her momma and—he had to admit—her daddy was in there too.

Lucy came into the room. "The doctor's calling in a prescription. Will you be all right if I go run and pick it up? Or should I have Sam do it?"

"They'll probably want insurance information. Why don't you take Sam with you to the pharmacy? And here—" He gently leaned forward and pulled his wallet out of his back pocket. "Here's your and Poppy's new insurance cards."

She opened her mouth to say something, then closed it and stood there blinking at him.

"Something wrong?" he asked.

Lucy didn't think Cal had ever been any sexier than he was in that moment, cradling his sick daughter and talking about things like insurance cards. The man she was looking at now was not the man who'd knocked her up and then thrown his secretary onto his desk. No, this was the kind of man who would stick around, the kind of man who loved and took care of his family.

"Thanks," she said around the tear-filled bubble in her throat. "I'll be back soon. Call me if you need anything."

"Will do."

She left the bedroom, knowing her daughter would be taken care of. Throughout her trip to the pharmacy with Sam she kept going over her decision to tell Cal about Poppy and what his reaction might be.

It was a strange and exhilarating feeling to have a potential partner to parent with. She'd been on her own for so long it was going to take her a while to adjust. She wondered how Cal would take the news that he was a father. Was he only enjoying playing at being a daddy, or was he developing feelings for his daughter? When he found out he was a daddy for real, would he stay around or would he leave?

She guessed the only way to be sure would be to tell him. Once it was out, she'd know where she stood and could make better decisions for her and Poppy. Either way they had their deal for a full year. By that time Poppy would be nearly two years old, and Lucy would have a tidy nest egg put away. She supposed she could ask Cal for child support if she had to. He'd pay to keep it hushed that he had a child if he didn't want Poppy in his life. If that was the case, they were no worse off than they were now.

It all seemed so logical. So why was she holding out the hope that Cal would want to keep fathering his daughter? And then the second, smaller hope that she and Cal would stay married and live happily ever after?

Now there was a dream.

She snorted, which drew Sam's attention in the car. "Something wrong, Mrs. Sellers?"

They were on their way home from the pharmacy. Lucy had picked up a few other things she thought she might need for Poppy.

"No. Just thinking. Can I ask you a question?"

"Sure."

"Do you have kids?"

He grinned. "Three. All boys."

"You like being a dad? I mean, it must be hard being away from them."

"Best thing I ever did, and yeah, it's hard. But when we're together, we're really together, you know?"

"Yeah." She didn't, but that wasn't something she wanted to burden Sam with.

She stayed quiet the rest of the ride home. When she got there, Cal was in the same spot and nearly the same position as he'd been in when she'd left, eyes closed.

"Hey," she whispered.

He opened his eyes. "Oh, hey. I fell asleep. Did you get the medicine?"

She held up the bag. "I hate to do it, but we should wake her up and give her a dose so it can start working right away."

He looked down at Poppy. "Isn't there some kind of superstition about waking a sleeping baby?"

"You want her in pain any longer than she has to be?"

"No." He gently nudged Poppy. "Hey, sweet pea, time to wake up and take your medicine. Come on, sweets." Poppy started howling. "Now I see why they say that," he said to Lucy and then turned Poppy so Lucy could drop the medicine into her mouth. "That's my girl. She took it like a champ. Now what?"

"Now you get her to go back to sleep."

"Easy." He rose, lifting Poppy to his shoulder, and walked.

It took only a few minutes before Poppy was asleep again. Cal laid her gently in her crib and backed away.

"Now what?" he asked.

"Now you come with me. I have something I need to talk with you about."

12

Lucy grabbed the baby monitor, led Cal into her bedroom, and closed the door. She'd been so calm in Poppy's room, but now alone here with Cal, she was a bundle of sweaty nerves. Where to start? Should she build up to it or blurt it out? How did people do things like this?

She wiped her hands on her skirt. "Have a seat." She gestured toward the two chairs by the fireplace.

He sat down and propped a booted foot on his knee. He had a big wet spot on his expensive dress shirt from Poppy's sweaty little body, his hair was messed up and his eyes were half-lidded and sleepy looking. If she hadn't been so twisted up inside from what she was about to tell him, she might've suggested option number eight or twenty-one. They were similar, but option eight added a twist she'd been dying to try and... She was stalling.

She lowered herself into the chair opposite him.

There was really no good way to say this so she just started.

"Back when we were together and I caught you with your secretary—"

"I said it before and I'll say it again—I'm sorry. And I'll keep on saying it until you believe it. I'm sorry."

"No, that wasn't what I wanted to talk about."

He shifted in his seat, dropping his foot to the floor and leaning in. "What is it that's got you so upset, darlin'? Is it Poppy? Is she worse off than you thought?"

"No, it's not that either. Be quiet a minute and let me get this out, okay?"

He nodded but kept watching her with an intensity that was so Cal.

"I left your office that day, and I swore to myself I'd never see you again. No matter what. And then things got very bad for me financially. If it were just me, I'd have sucked it up, been homeless or gone to live in a shelter or something, but I had Poppy to think of. So I put my pride aside and I went to you for a job. I never expected..." her hand fluttered in a helpless motion, "... that you'd offer me marriage. I figured I had a fifty-fifty shot at getting my old job back. The odds were high enough that I had to ask. For Poppy.

"And then Kevin came back." Her eyes began to fill with tears, but she held them at bay. Cal started to say something, but she stopped him with her hand. "It was...still is a life-or-death situation. And again, if it were just me, I'd deal with him however I could, but there was Poppy. He only wants her now because she's the key he uses to get to me. He can't have children of his own, so he was willing to marry me. I thought I was doing what was best for everyone. He agreed to pass Poppy off as his own. But she's not. Kevin isn't Poppy's father. You are."

He was quiet so long, his expression unchanged, she grew nervous, waiting for an explosion that never came. "Aren't you going to say something?"

"Darlin', I know how to do math."

"What are you talking about?"

"I knew she had to be mine by the timing. Unless you were cheating on me, which I couldn't complain about, now could I? I figured she had to be mine. I am much relieved to know you didn't cheat and that she really, truly is mine."

She shook her head. "I don't understand. You *knew*? Why didn't you ever say anything? Why didn't you *do* anything?"

"What could I do? You married that asshole instead of telling me. Your thoughts on the matter couldn't be any plainer. You made it clear you didn't want me in your life let alone Poppy's life after what I did to you. And rightly so from where I was standing at the time. But I kept tabs and helped when I could. I paid for that private room and your expenses when she was born. She has a trust fund and a college fund. She is also listed as one of the heirs in my will, the main heir. I did what I could for her from the outside."

Her heart was pounding so hard she couldn't catch her breath. He knew. All this time. All the while she was taking the beatings from Kevin, he knew Poppy was his daughter.

He scooted forward in his chair. "But now I know her. I've held her and rocked her. She's mine, and I'm claiming her. I won't allow another day to go by in her life without me in it. I'm here, and I'm not leaving."

"So that's it. Everything's solved in your world."

"No, everything's not solved, but it's starting to work itself out."

"What about a year from now when this marriage is over and we go our separate ways?"

"If that's what you want, then that's what we'll do. If it was up to me, I'd make you my wife in every way—not just in name—and the three of us would be a family."

"Why?"

"Well, I thought that was fairly obvious."

"*Obviously* not."

"I'm in love with you." He said it so simply when nothing that had ever happened between them could ever be classified as simple, including her very complicated feelings for him.

"It took you walking out of my life and into the arms of another man for me to realize it. And I swore —" he took her hands in his, "—that if I ever got another chance with you, I'd do everything I could to be the kind of man you can trust and maybe love in return. And then you walked into my office in your tight blouse and even tighter skirt, flipping your hair over your shoulder, all but demanding that I give you your old job, and I knew. That was my second chance, maybe my only chance to have you back again.

"I know it's going to take time to earn your trust and

forgiveness. Seeing you with that other man, imagining you with him, watching you create a family with him... I got back some of what I must have put you through, and it nearly brought me to my knees. In one stupid, thoughtless act I lost you and my daughter. I lost everything that mattered before I even knew it could matter. So now here I am getting to know my daughter and wooing my wife. And hoping I can win her back."

"I don't know what to say."

She truly didn't. His declaration left her speechless. Maybe there was such a thing as second chances and do-overs. If he'd been anything in the past few weeks, he'd been consistent, putting his words into action over and over. It was clear he adored his daughter, doting on her and stepping up to be a real father to her. Maybe they could work things out. Maybe she could trust him. Maybe, maybe, maybe.

"You don't need to say anything."

"But I do. When you talk like that, Cal, you make me want everything you said. You make me want to trust you again."

He grinned like he'd been awarded a prize. "I want to kiss you so bad right now, darlin', that I don't think I could stop once I started."

"I'm not sure I'd want you to if you did. Come here, cowboy." She grabbed him by his still-damp shirt collar. "Kiss me."

Cal put his lips to hers. This kiss was like none they'd ever shared. Their first kisses had been feverish and hungry, their recent kisses had been tentative and testing, but this kiss...this kiss was sure and hopeful, and it outshone any other kiss. He dropped to his knees in front of her chair and brought her right up against his body, her legs on either side of his hips. The feel of her... There was no holding back. He let his hands wander, relearning her curves.

He trailed a line of kisses across her jaw and down her neck. She sifted her fingers through his hair and held him as though she never wanted him to stop. He made thorough work of kissing her, setting everything free that he'd kept pent up. He wanted her more than he'd ever wanted a woman in his life, more than the first time he'd had her. This was *the* first, the most important first. She was letting him back into her heart and maybe her body. He grew wild for her, desperate for the feel of skin on skin and her hands on his body.

Gripping her ass, he rocked against her. She worked at the buttons of his shirt. He followed suit, undoing the buttons of her blouse, exposing her an inch at a time until he was looking down at the creamy swell of her breasts spilling out of the cups of her bra.

He bent his head to her beckoning flesh, cupping her breasts in both hands. She'd always been more than a handful, but now after having his child, her body had become a lush wonderland of new curves to explore. God, he wanted her. He pressed his erection against her so she could see for herself how much. She answered with a moan and dug her heels into his backside, grinding against him.

He peeled back a cup of her bra and then the other, and her breasts popped free from their confines. Bending back, she guided him to where she wanted him. He was only happy to oblige, drawing her nipple into his mouth and sucking hard.

"Ahh," she gasped.

He wanted to be inside her so bad he thought he'd die before he'd get the chance. Slipping a hand between her legs, he felt how wet she was through her panties. He had to touch her, dip his fingers into her slickness. He slid his hand into the waistband of her panties, stroking into her with one then two fingers. She arched back farther as he worked her, drawing out her pleasure toward orgasm.

She began panting, and he knew she was close, so close. He drove his fingers into her as he wanted to drive his cock into her, over and over, not letting up until she broke on a low moan, clutching his head to her breast. He nuzzled her, working his way back to her mouth, and kissed her, a long, slow promise that this was only the beginning. There would be more, so much more between them.

"Cal?"

"Hmm," he answered as he kissed the slopes of her breasts.

"That wasn't in the option agreement."

"We'll add it." He moved his fingers inside her again. "How about number five? I'm feeling number five real strong, darlin'."

"Five?" She gasped.

"It's the one where I put my mouth where my hand is now."

"No. Just your hands. I want your mouth here and

here." She cupped one breast and then the other, rolling her nipples between her thumbs and fingers.

"Jesus, darlin'," he breathed.

He gripped her panties and ripped them in half, exposing her. Running his hands up her pale thighs, he couldn't believe what a lucky bastard he was to have her wanting and willing. He widened her legs, using both hands on her, rubbing her clit and stroking her deep. Gazing up at her, he touched his tongue to her nipple. Her arousal was intoxicating, and he couldn't stop watching her reactions as he pleasured her. The sounds she made, the scent of her, he was sure he would come right here with his mouth on her and her hand in his hair, urging him on.

She brought her other hand up to her breast and rubbed her nipple. The first gasps of her impending orgasm drove him mad. This was his Lucy, wild and wanton and so uninhibited. He picked up the pace, slipping three fingers inside of her and working her until her hand fisted in his hair and she cried out.

He slid his fingers out of her and laid his head on her stomach. His dick throbbed so hard he thought it might explode any minute. If he touched her again, he'd lose it for sure. He couldn't hear her moan one more time without being inside her.

This time wasn't for him though. It was for her. He wanted to show her what he couldn't say, that he hadn't had a woman since he'd had her. That he'd loved her when he'd cheated on her, but instead of telling her, he'd sabotaged it because it scared the hell out of him. She scared the hell out of him. Her and her power to make him drop to his knees and beg her to take him back. And that he was weak, so very weak when it came to her.

He'd known about his daughter, but instead of doing what he normally would—barge in and take over everything—he'd let her go, thinking that was best for her and her mother. He'd thought about Poppy a lot, wondering what she looked like, how she was growing and if she was happy.

He hadn't lied when he'd told Lucy that he wanted his daughter. Whatever happened between the two of them, he'd be in Poppy's life. He wasn't letting her go. Ever.

Lucy stirred, sifting her fingers through his hair and scattering goose bumps over his skin. "Are we going to take this to the bed?"

He looked up at her, past her breasts spilling out of their cups, and he wanted to answer yes. God, yes. "I think," he said, kissing each of her breasts, "that we've made a very good dent in the options."

"What about you?" She tried to reach down and grab him, but he moved before she could put a hand on him.

"My pleasure, darlin', was in pleasuring you..." he ran a finger over one breast then the other, "...and finally seeing these..." he bent and licked one of her nipples and she shuddered, "...and putting my hands and mouth on them."

"But don't you want to have sex?"

"There isn't anything I want more in this world. And I mean *anything*."

She scooted up, trying to pull her skirt back down. "I don't understand."

The old him would've nailed her to the chair, but the new him wanted her to want him as much if not more than he wanted her. For that he would wait. Even if it killed him.

He stilled her efforts. "Do you know how incredibly sexy you are all laid out like a feast for a king? I could look at you like this all day long."

"But you don't want to have sex with me. Is this some kind of game?"

"I'm not playing here." He took her hand and put it on his crotch. "Does this feel like a game to you?"

She moved her hand up and down, and he had to grab it between both of his to get her to stop. "Darlin', if you do that, I'm going to embarrass myself."

She retracted her hand and went back to putting her clothes to rights. "I don't understand you, Cal Sellers. I don't understand what this is or what you want from me."

"Did I leave you wanting? Because if I did, then you should shove your skirt back up, and I'll make you come so hard the staff will think I'm killing you up here." He rose onto his knees and bracketed her with his hands on the arms of the chair. "Don't think for one second, Lucy, that I don't want to fuck you into next week. And then when I'm done, fuck you again and again until my name is the only thing you say and my face is the only one you connect with pleasure."

She gasped, her eyes widening, and he thought for a moment that he'd scared her with his intensity. But no, she was *excited*. Her full breasts heaved, and her cheeks were flushed. She watched him with the same hunger he felt for her. Oh yeah, she was turned on.

"I'm going to think about the sound and feel of you as I jerk off tonight. And then tomorrow and the next day and the day after that, however long it takes until you trust me completely, I'm going to walk across the hall to your room and make you come over and over again. And then I'm going to go back to my room and get off on everything I've done to you. When the day comes that you trust me, that you truly believe I've changed, that's the night I'm going to take you to bed and make you my wife."

13

Every night for nearly a week, Cal had gone to Lucy's room and gotten her off in increasingly inventive ways. Then, just as he'd said he would, he'd gone back to his room and jacked off, remembering everything he'd done to her. This had seemed like a really good idea when he'd originally come up with it. But the memory of Lucy naked, legs spread, her face flushed, and lips parted chased him into the days. More than once he'd gone into his private bathroom in his office and gotten off thinking about the way she looked and the sounds she made when she came.

Tonight he had something special planned for her. Owning a company that sold adult toys had never been handier than it had in the past couple of days. One of the boxes he'd stuffed inside his briefcase for her contained something he wasn't sure she'd ever considered trying. Which made him want to try it all the more.

He found Lucy playing with their daughter on the living room floor, where Lucy helped Poppy pound colorful balls with a hammer until they dropped into holes, rolled down shoots, and popped back out again, eliciting a shriek of joy from Poppy. Dropping his briefcase on the couch, he sat on the floor next to his two favorite girls.

He bent and kissed the top of Poppy's head. "Hey there, sweet pea." Then he gave Lucy a long, lingering kiss. "Hello, darlin'."

She blushed and dropped her gaze to her lap. So she'd thought about him while he'd been gone, or at least the things he'd done to her the night before. He'd been quite inventive, if he did say so himself. It hadn't been a hardship to research different ways to pleasure a woman. He thought he'd been experienced in it before, but now every night with Lucy had been like a master class in getting a woman off, and he hadn't even scratched the surface of all there was to know and do.

"Hi," she said, her blush deepening. "I wanted to talk to you before dinner and Poppy's bedtime ritual."

"Go on."

"You don't have to come to my room tonight."

He frowned, his mood turning. He'd already failed in wooing his wife, and it hadn't even been a week. Where had he gone wrong?

"If that's what you want," he said, flattening his voice so she wouldn't hear his disappointment.

She watched him closely from under her lashes, her body stiff as though she was bracing for something. "It's just that I got my period today, and I'm not really feeling like doing, you know, things."

Oh, was that all? He suppressed a relieved sigh and leaned in to kiss her cheek. "Not to worry. Is there anything I can do for you, darlin'? Are you feeling very sickly?"

"I'm okay."

She kept watching him in that odd way, and then it hit him. She was expecting him to react the way her ex would. It brought back the memory of the night she'd agreed to marry him and her insisting on adding the last option to their option agreement, the one that made everything in it totally and completely optional. Goddammit. She was probably going to be on pins and needles the rest of the night, wondering if he'd keep his word or not, wondering if he was going to force himself on her. Fucking hell. His chest tightened, thinking of everything she'd been through, and it got hard to breathe, like he'd been punched in the gut.

He traced the barely there bruise under her eye. He wanted her to remember the difference between him and her ex. He would cut off his own hand before he'd ever put a mark on her like that asshole had.

"This is almost gone. I'll be glad when I can look at you and not see what that bastard put you through. I only hope one day you can look at me and not expect me to turn on you like he did."

"I don't."

"No, darlin', you do. But that's okay. It's part of your healing and the trust we're building between us."

"I don't know what to say when you say things like that to me."

"There's nothing that needs to be said." With his finger he stroked from her temple to cheek. "Eventually you'll just know..." he put his hand over her heart, "...and feel, and nothing will ever have to be said because it will just be. I'm not like him. I might hurt you in other ways, but I'll never hurt you physically, and I'll never, ever force myself on you."

"I know that. Don't be ridiculous."

He could've chased her denial until he cornered her and forced her to admit what she could hardly admit to herself, but that wouldn't get them anywhere. So he changed the subject.

"I brought you a present." He grabbed his briefcase.

"You don't have to get me things."

"This is really for me, but I'm hoping you'll like it too." He opened the case and pulled out the *other* present he'd brought home for her.

"Cal, you did not get me a gun."

"I did, darlin', and I arranged for you to have lessons on how to load it, clean it, and shoot it. I want you to be able to protect yourself." He'd wanted to give it to her sooner, but it had taken awhile to find the right teacher for her, someone who would be discreet and understanding of their situation.

"I don't want a gun in the house with Poppy. What if she gets a hold of it?"

"Well, that will be part of your lessons—proper handling and safety."

She thrust it back at him. "No."

Instead of taking the box from her, he picked up their daughter and sat her on his lap. "I understand your position. I really do. But let me ask you this—what if Kevin gets in here again? What if I'm not home and Sam's not here? What if he gets past our security and there's no one to protect you—to protect Poppy—except you? How will you do it? Because I'm telling you, darlin', if that asshole gets in here, I want you to be able to put a bullet in him."

Lucy looked down at the box in her shaking hands and couldn't come up with an argument against it. If she'd had a gun the last time she saw Kevin, she would've used it. In a minute. Without a thought. She'd have shot him and kept on shooting him until she ran out of bullets, and then she'd beat him with the gun until her arm got too tired to swing anymore.

She clutched the gun to her chest. "When's my first lesson?"

"That's my girl. And this is my girl," he said to Poppy as he lifted her above his head, making her giggle.

Poppy sure did adore her daddy and had pretty much from day one. Cal had taken to fatherhood as though he'd never missed a day in her life. More than once Lucy had wondered what would've happened if she'd told Cal about her pregnancy when she'd found out she was expecting. Where would they be right now? Would they have gotten back together? Did Cal resent her for the months he'd spent away from his daughter? Did he regret not being there for her birth?

"When's dinner?" Cal asked, drawing her out of her musings.

"In about fifteen minutes."

"I'm going to change and come back down to play with Poppy." He sat Poppy back down and put the hammer in her hand. She immediately went back to whacking a ball into the hole.

"And that's what I'm going to do when boys come knocking on my front door wanting to court you. Thump them upside the head." He ruffled Poppy's hair and then went upstairs to change.

Lucy couldn't help but stare at him as he walked away. The backside of Cal was one of her very favorite sides of him. She blushed all over again, remembering of all the things he'd done to her over the past several days. And not once had he asked for anything in return or made a move to do more than see to her pleasure. If she was honest, she'd admit that there'd been times when she wished he'd drop his pants and drive into her. She missed the feel of him on top of her and the way he'd watch as he thrust in and out of her.

She shook her head to stop those thoughts. She'd only frustrate herself since he wouldn't be visiting her tonight. She rubbed her tummy. Her cramps had gotten worse after having Poppy. The over-the-counter pain meds helped but didn't take away all the pain.

She thought about what Cal had said, that she expected him to behave like Kevin had. He'd conditioned her to expect the worst, and she'd usually been right. Kevin hadn't cared if she was on her period, sick, or if she was in the mood. When she'd been on her period, he'd force her facedown on the bed or wherever they happened to be and did what he wanted. It had gotten to where she'd hated sex. Even when she hadn't resisted, Kevin had still managed to make her feel ashamed and dirty.

He'd complained about how fat she'd gotten after having Poppy, pinching her breasts and the rolls at her waist. She'd tried really hard to be a good wife to him, to be quiet and timid the way he liked. She'd dressed in the clothes he preferred and worn her hair the way he wanted her to. And it was never enough. The slightest thing would set him off, and then he'd start in on what a horrible wife and mother she was. The insults quickly escalated to threats. If she didn't move fast enough or address him with respect, he'd grab her and shake her, twist her arm behind her back or smack her around.

He *enjoyed* hitting her. When he'd come around later with his apologies, it was the look on his face as he'd hit her that helped her remember how much he loved to hurt her. She accepted his apologies and promises to never do it again, knowing he didn't mean them. Hit, blame, apologize. Over and over they repeated the same cycle. Until she'd finally gotten out.

She glanced at the box in her lap. She'd like to see the look on Kevin's face when she pulled a gun on him. She'd like to humiliate him and make him suffer the way he'd humiliated and hurt her. And then she'd put the gun to his head and blow his brains out. Just thinking about it brought a smile to her face.

Poppy crawled over and whacked the box with her hammer.

"No, no, sweet girl. No whacking mommy."

Cal came back into the room. "She's aggressive. I like that." He lay down on his belly on the floor to be eye level with Poppy. "But no hitting people. Unless they're boys wanting to take liberties before they've put a ring on your finger and made you their wife. Maybe not even then."

"I think having a daughter is karmic retribution for all of the liberties you've taken with women who weren't your wife."

"I think you're right. Add to it that my wife is the only woman I want to take liberties with and it's definitely ironic if not some kind of retribution."

"With all the ironic karmic retribution you've racked up, you're bound to have only daughters and no sons."

"As long as I'm having them with you, darlin', I don't care which I have." He grabbed a ball that had gotten away from Poppy and handed it back to her. "Here you go, sweet pea. I'd have ten daughters if they all came out looking like you," he told Poppy.

Lucy snorted. "You say that because she looks exactly like you."

"You think? I think she looks like her pretty momma."

"The only thing she got from me was my grandma's red hair."

"Nah, she's every inch you."

"Thank you for the gun."

He glanced up at her. "I'd rather give you diamonds or pearls, but that's not what you need."

"Is it wrong that I hope I get a chance to use it?"

"No, but honestly, darlin', I hope you don't. I hope that bastard stays locked up where he can't get to you or Poppy."

"Still." She lifted the lid of the box and was surprised at how utilitarian the gun looked. "It's kind of ugly."

"But effective, and that's what we're going for here."

She lifted it out of the box, weighing it in her hand. "Not as heavy as I thought it would be."

"Easy there." He pushed the nozzle away. "First lesson in gun handling is to assume the gun's always loaded. It's not, but if you approach every gun as if it was, you'll be much safer."

She gripped it in both hands and aimed at an ugly vase across the room, resting her finger lightly on the trigger.

"Now that's about the sexiest thing I've ever seen," he said.

"I'm not going for sexy, I'm going for scary."

"Scary sexy then."

She sighed and put the gun back in the box. "Maybe I'll be more frightening once I've had lessons."

"No doubt."

14

C al hung up the phone and let out a string of curses. Kevin Walker was free on a technicality. Free to come after Lucy and Poppy. Goddammit. He poured himself another whiskey. He hated having to tell Lucy she was back to looking over her shoulder and worrying about when and where that asshole would show up next.

Taking a sip of his drink, he leaned back in his chair to think. Lucy would start her lessons tomorrow, and the security measures he'd ordered from Lucas's company were in place, including an extra bodyguard inside the house and a patrol outside. What else could he do to protect his family?

His family. A few weeks into his marriage and he was already counting on it holding. He was crazy in love with his wife and crazy in love with his daughter and pretty sure he was just plain old crazy for having thrown it all away the first time around. This was his second chance, and he wasn't going to blow it.

He downed the rest of his drink. He couldn't wait for the time when Lucy slept beside him every night like a real married couple. The visits to her room had been fun, but there was something missing from their encounters. It was more than Lucy's fears and lack of trust, it was something deeper, something just beyond his reach.

He headed for the stairs and bed, checking in on Poppy as part of his new routine. She was curled up on her side, her little fist in her mouth. As he'd done so many times before, he thanked God for her and Lucy. They'd brought more to his life than he'd ever expected and turned his house into a real home. His world had been redrawn and colored. It was full in a way it had never been before. He didn't think he could ever go back to living without them.

Easing the door closed, he turned toward Lucy's closed door. He'd gotten used to being with her before turning in for the night. It was more than a physical thing between them. He'd already confessed his love for her, and even though she didn't say it, he had an inkling she might feel the same. As with every thing between them, it was going to take some time and effort, but it was worth it. They were worth it.

He went to his room and made a valiant attempt to sleep. Although he'd slept in his own bed every night after visiting Lucy, tonight it felt big and empty, and he didn't have the smell of her on him or the memories of being with her to help him slip into slumber.

She'd made it clear that she didn't want him to visit

her tonight. Their relationship was at a tipping point. She was starting to trust him and maybe even rely on him a little. While the sexual play between them had been hot, they left him feeling incomplete. It had nothing to do with his lack of physical release. He wanted more, something deeper. He'd give anything to have her snuggled up next to him right now. After a few more minutes he gave up and made the trek down the hall past Poppy's room.

He knocked on Lucy's door and waited for her to let him in. It was a little like looking over the edge of a cliff right before he jumped off. Maybe the bungee cord would hold and she'd let him in or else it would snap and she'd shut the door in his face.

The door cracked open and Lucy appeared, wearing plaid, flannel pajama pants and an oversized T-shirt. With no bra.

"Yes?" she asked.

"Can I come in?"

"Cal, I told you I'm not feeling well. Maybe in a few days."

"Is there anything you need?"

"No. I'll be fine. I just need some sleep."

"That's why I'm here. To sleep. That's all I have in mind tonight. I promise. It seems as though I've grown used to being with you."

Lucy watched him, rubbing her crossed arms. "You're drunk."

"I'm not drunk. I had a drink."

"I really just want to be alone. Can't you understand that?"

"If that's what you want, darlin'." He started to turn away.

"Wait."

He held his breath, watching her face as a myriad of emotions moved across it. He'd give anything to know what she was thinking. Would she take a chance and trust him? Had he shown her enough times in enough ways that she could?

"I can't give you want you want," she said.

"All I want to do is sleep with you. Sleep as in close my eyes and snore and when I wake up in the morning see your beautiful face on the other pillow."

She eyeballed him for a few seconds more before she gave a short nod. "Sleep. And that's all."

He would've whooped if he didn't think it would get him kicked out of her room. "That's all I've got planned." He walked to the foot of the bed. "Which side do you prefer?"

"This one." She went to stand on the side closest to the door.

He went to the opposite side of the bed. "Good choice."

This felt like a moment for them, one of those little things that changed everything after it. They both climbed in on their respective sides. He turned toward her, but she faced away, so he eased up behind her and put his arm around her.

Her whole body went tense, and it was as though her breathing had stilled too. He snuggled deeper into her, and she let out a sound he'd never heard her make before. Instantly he backed away to his side of the bed.

"What did I do?" he asked.

"Nothing."

"That was not a nothing response to a little cuddling."

"I don't like it...like that."

"You don't like cuddling like that?"

"I don't like anyone behind me." She scooted closer to the edge away from him.

He rolled to his back and stared up at the ceiling. It took a moment for him to think about what she'd said and not said. With Lucy it was one clue wrapped in a thousand layers of things she couldn't bring herself to say. She didn't like it like that with someone behind her. He suspected she wasn't talking about cuddling. She was talking about sex and sex in that position. He sifted through some of his most amazing memories of doing it with Lucy just that way, including one of the first times they'd been together. She'd liked it then, but now...

He turned his head and looked at her stiff form, curled up in a ball, clinging to the edge of the bed. This wasn't what he had in mind when he'd imagined sleeping with his wife tonight.

"Lucy?"

"What?"

"Will you turn over and look at me?"

"Either go to sleep or leave."

He took a deep breath. He couldn't put the question out of his mind, but at the same time he dreaded the answer. "Lucy, what did he do to you?"

"You know what he did. You saw the photos. And you saw firsthand what he can do."

"Why can't I cuddle you from behind?"

"Damn it, Cal. Shut up and go to sleep."

"Did he make you do things you didn't want to do? Sexual things?"

"Why do you want to hear about it? Is this something you're going to get off on later?"

He put a hand on her shoulder to try to get her to roll toward him. "I think you should go see a counselor, someone you can talk to."

"I don't want to talk about it."

"You'll never get past it if you don't."

"Stop pushing me on this."

"Darlin'—"

She whipped toward him so fast he jerked back. "You want to hear about how he raped me? Or how when he wasn't raping me, he was sodomizing me or making me suck him off? You want to hear about how it didn't matter what I did or didn't do, I would always have to put up with him sticking his dick in me whenever he felt like it? You want to hear about the time he made me strip naked in front of his friend and how he held me by the hair while he did me from behind and his friend stuck his dick in my mouth?

"You want to hear about the *other* photos he took of me? You want to know how he threatened to kill Poppy if I didn't do what he said? Or how he locked me in the house every day with no money, no phone, and no way out? You want to hear about how sometimes he liked to tie me up and—"

"Stop!"

"No, you wanted to hear about it, Cal, so here it is. All of the ugliness. He especially liked to force me face-down on the bed or the floor with my arm twisted behind my back—"

"No more, Lucy."

"That's why I don't like anyone behind me, cuddling or otherwise. You're just going to have to live with that and get over your hurt little feelings." She flopped back over and sucked in a sharp-sounding breath.

He lay there listening to her trying not to cry, his chest aching like he'd been punched in the solar plexus, feeling like the biggest ass in the world. He'd had no idea. No fucking idea at all about what she'd been through. He thought he knew, but his imaginings didn't come close to her reality.

He swiped at his eyes and climbed out of bed. What was he doing here, playing at being a husband to her? He knew nothing of her or how to help her. All the while he'd been thinking only of what he wanted, painting an image of them getting over Lucy's past like it was some little bump in the road. She'd been brutalized and raped. He didn't know anything about that, couldn't even come close to imagining it. All of his money, his power, his success was nothing, meant nothing.

He went down on his knees next to her. "I'm sorry." His useless platitude boomeranged around her and came back at him, echoing hollowly in his head. He cleared his throat and tried again. "What can I do?"

"Nothing. Go to bed." Her words were flat and unforgiving.

He laid his forehead on the edge of the bed. "Let me do something for you."

"There's nothing to do. It's already done."

He punched the mattress. Useless. He was totally useless to her. There was no fixing this for her. All of the money in the world couldn't take away everything she'd lived through.

He found her hand and slipped it into his. "You're safe here. You and Poppy will always be safe here. No matter what happens between us, you will always have a safe home. I promise you. You'll never have to be afraid again." He kissed the back of her hand and tucked it under her chin. "Good night." He started from the room.

Her hand snaked out and grabbed his leg. "Don't leave me."

The last thing she needed was another man, especially one as worthless and idiotic as him. "Lucy..."

"I've never told anyone any of that."

"Why did you tell me?"

"Because you asked. No one ever asked, they just assumed. He looks so normal. No one would ever believe."

"I believe."

She moved over to make room for him next to her. "Don't leave me."

How could he? How could he ever leave her alone and defenseless against that monster again? He got between the covers, careful not to touch her or move in any way that she might consider a threat. But then she did something so wholly unexpected it made his breath catch. She picked up his arm and put it around her, laying her head on his shoulder and snuggling up next to him. Why would she seek the touch and closeness of a man after what she'd experienced?

"Now you're going to treat me differently, aren't you?" she asked.

He shook his head, unable to get words past the clog in his throat.

"Liar."

Lucy wished she'd never said anything about what Kevin had done to her. She'd told Cal the worst of what had happened to her physically, but there were no words for what it had done to her on the inside. The past few weeks with Cal were the most normal—or as close to what she remembered of normal—she'd felt in a long time.

She disgusted him now. She knew it by the way he held himself away from her and how he wouldn't look her in the eye. He'd never see her as the Lucy she'd been before. He'd never flirt with her or touch her without thinking about what she'd been through.

"Kiss me," she dared. It felt as though everything between them was riding on what he would do next.

"Darlin'..."

She leaned up and looked down at him in challenge. "Do it. Prove to me that you don't see me differently now. An hour ago I wouldn't have had to beg you. You would've had me flat on my back, pressing your erection against my leg and making me feel how much you want me."

"I don't think—"

"That's the problem. You're thinking. I don't want thinking Cal. I want hornier-than-hell Cal. I want the Cal who pushed my skirt up and made me feel like a woman, not a victim."

Lucy slipped her hand in his shorts and stroked his flaccid penis.

He grabbed her wrist. "Don't."

"Cal, I want to."

"No."

She yanked her hand out of his pants, ashamed of her desperation and of what must think about her now. He didn't even want her to touch him. Would he ever look at her the way he used to? Or would he always see what she'd been through?

His gaze locked on to hers. "When I knocked on your door, I made a promise to you—no sex. Just sleep. I intend to keep that promise, Lucy, and not because of what you told me."

"I don't believe you."

"Believe this—I want you. Every minute of every day. What I don't want is for you to ever feel as though you have to service me."

"That's not what—"

"No? When I walked in here, you were very clear about what you wanted and what you didn't want. I'm pretty sure giving me a hand job wasn't on your want list." His tone softened as he stroked her cheek. "You want to know what I see when I look at you?"

She nodded.

"I see a strong, beautiful woman who went through hell and back. I see my wife and the mother of my child. I see a woman who has no idea how incredibly sexy she is. You have more power than you realize. He left you memories you don't know what to do with, but he didn't take anything from you. Not as far as I can see."

"You're just saying that."

"No. I'm not. You might not believe me now, but someday you will." He leaned in slowly and brushed a kiss across her lips. "I think it's time we do that thing I promised and go to sleep. Poppy will be waking up in a few hours."

He held out his arms for her, and she snuggled into his side with her head on his chest.

He turned out the light. "I love you."

She couldn't move, afraid to break whatever spell Cal was under. Of all the things he'd ever said to her, what he'd just proclaimed had to be the most hopeful thing she'd ever heard. She felt the weight of his words like a blanket wrapping itself around her and working through the cracks in the walls she'd built just to survive another day. He loved her. He really, truly loved her.

After a few moments his breathing evened out. He was asleep, so it was safe to say what she'd wanted to tell him for days.

"I love you too, Cal Sellers," she whispered.

She could've sworn she felt him smile in the darkness.

15

Over the next week Cal came to her room each night, knocked on her door, and waited for her to open it and invite him in. Lucy had gotten used to sleeping in his arms. She'd taken him into her body just about every way, but somehow taking him into her bed felt more intimate than any of the sexual stuff they'd ever done. By the end of the week she was ready to once again renew their sexual relationship.

So when he knocked on her door that night, she answered it completely naked. His mouth fell open, and he stared at her.

"Are you going to come in or not?" she asked, trying hard not to feel insecure.

Cal hadn't seen her fully naked since she had Poppy. There were other changes to her body like the burn on her shoulder and the scar on her hip where she'd gotten cut when Kevin had pushed her down and she hit the corner of the glass coffee table, breaking it.

If she'd answered the door to him fully dressed, she might have chickened out.

He moved so fast into the room he created a breeze. She closed the door and leaned back against it, trying to strike a seductive pose, but she wasn't all that sure she pulled it off. He was still staring at her as though he couldn't stop. He *liked* what he saw. That revelation gave her courage she couldn't have mustered on her own.

"I was thinking," she said, sauntering toward him, "that we'd try option number forty-seven."

He bobbed his head.

"You don't have any idea what option number forty-seven is, do you?"

"No, but I like the way it starts out."

His words emboldened her further. "So I could tell you that it's the one where you stand on your head—"

"There's an option where I stand on my head?" He shook his head. "Never mind. I don't care." He shucked his boxer shorts and stood before her, ready for any option. "Where do you want me?"

"On the bed."

He backed up, never taking his eyes off her, until his calves hit the edge of the bed. He sat down. "Now what?"

She walked toward him, adding a little extra bounce to her step that made her breasts jiggle. He seemed to like that. A lot.

"Jesus, darlin'," he breathed, his gaze focused on her chest.

"Number forty-seven is the one where we can't use our hands."

He looked up at her then. "No hands? At all? What if I want my hands here?" He put his palms up as if to cup her breasts. She felt it as though he'd actually touched her. "What if I want to slide my fingers here?" He turned one hand and made a forward motion with two fingers pretending to stroke into her with them. She clenched her thighs together, his phantom touch making her throb for the real thing.

She put a knee on the mattress between his legs and grabbed her breasts, presenting them to him. "Are you saying that you only want to use your hands on these? I'm disappointed in you, cowboy. I thought you were more creative than that."

He leaned forward, his gaze on hers, and licked one of her nipples, giving her an exquisite chill. "Oh, darlin', if this is a challenge, I'm up for it."

"Mmm." She raised her knee, stroking up then down the length of him, eliciting a groan from him. "I see how up you are."

"Shall we make a wager?"

"On what?"

"Who will use their hands first."

"What's the wager?"

He leaned in and licked a circle around her belly button. She was already wet and dying for his hands on her, and they hadn't even kissed yet.

"Winner gets to pick the next ten options," he answered.

"Five."

He glanced up at her and traced the under slope of her breast with his tongue. She sucked in a breath.

"Not very confident, are you?" he asked.

"No, I'm curious to find out which option you'll choose first. I don't want to wait ten nights to find out."

"Darlin', I'd be glad to do all ten of your options tonight."

"Now who's not very confident they'll win?"

"Even the loser wins in this bargain."

She bent down, forcing him to lie back, and placed her hands on the bed on either side of him. Brushing her nipples up the length of his body from groin to chest, she answered, "True. It's a win/win wager."

"Jesus, darlin'. Do that again."

She obliged, pressing her breasts together and stroking his penis with them. He stacked his hands behind his head and watched her. On the third downward stroke she licked the head, swirling her tongue around it. He moaned and started to reach for her, but pulled the gesture before he touched her.

"Come here, darlin'. I want to kiss you."

"Mmm, not yet." She worked him some more until his hips lifted off the bed and he growled at her to stop. "What? Don't you like what I'm doing?"

"I want to be inside you when I come."

"But you were just bragging about doing it ten times tonight."

"I lied."

He somehow made a move with his legs that flipped her onto the bed next to him. In a second he was on her, pressing the full length of his body to hers, his mouth covering hers in a kiss that let her know how much he wanted her. She wrapped her legs around him, bringing him right where she wanted him most. He changed the angle of the kiss, and suddenly she was hot and desperate for the feel of him inside of her. She pressed her hips up then down, rubbing her clit against him. Close, so close.

He pulled his mouth from hers and looked down at her. "This is the stupidest option on the list. I want to touch you so bad. Here..." he rocked his hips, sliding himself against her slickness, "...and here." He bent his head and drew one of her nipples deep into his mouth.

She fisted the sheets as he kept up the pace and then she came, her arms going around him and holding him to her.

"You lost," he said, a self-satisfied smile lighting up his face. He rocked back and thrust all the way into her.

She froze, then pushed at him. "Get out! Get out of me!"

It took Cal a second to comprehend what she was saying. He was finally inside her, finally home. When her words hit, he pulled out of her and backed away, up and off her entirely until he was standing beside the bed looking down at her panicked face.

"What?" he asked. He'd been right there. What had he done wrong?

"You can't be inside of me like that."

Putting his hands on his hips and closing his eyes, he took a deep breath. In, then out, until he felt like he had some kind of control over himself and wouldn't jump back on top of her.

"Okay," he said after a while. "We don't have to do

this." But Jesus God he wanted to. More deep breathing.

She moved...to the other side of the bed. The cold hand of despair reached down inside of him and fisted in his chest. He'd screwed this up. She'd trusted him and he blew it. Completely. He'd never get her trust back. He realized she'd pulled something out of the nightstand drawer and was handing it to him.

"—this on," she said.

He looked at what was in her hand. A condom. She wanted him to wear a condom. Relief flooded him first. He hadn't totally fucked this up. And then confusion set in. What in the hell?

"Why do I have to wear a condom? There hasn't been anyone else since you."

She withdrew her hand with the condom, and he could've hit himself upside the head for his stupidity. He should've just put the damn thing on and asked her about it later.

She got very nervous then, crossing her arms over her body. "I'm not going to be totally in the clear for another two months. Anyone I'm with has to wear one."

He couldn't wrap his head around what she was getting at. "Clear of what? Aren't you on the Pill or something?"

"Yes, but the Pill doesn't protect against HIV."

She said it like he was stupid or something, which at the moment he sort of was. And then it hit him, and he took a step back.

"Your son-of-a-bitch ex gave you HIV?"

"No. I don't know. I won't know for a while. I'm not in the clear yet. Neither is Poppy."

"Poppy...?" He reached a hand out to the bedpost.

"He was with his other wives. And while I was pregnant..."

She let that hang in the air between them. All of a sudden his legs wouldn't hold him anymore, and he collapsed onto the bed. Dropping his head into his hands, he cursed her ex and this whole fucking situation.

"I'm sorry," she said.

He could hear the anguish in her voice. None of this was her fault, and yet here she was paying the price. His idiocy in his office had led to this. All of it could be laid at his door. Once again she'd left him speechless and with the overwhelming feeling that nothing between them would ever be fixed. It certainly would never be the same as it had been *before*.

Before he'd thought himself cock of the block and thrown her away like she was nothing. Before she'd found out she was pregnant with his child. Before she'd married that bastard who had done unspeakable things to her.

"I wish you would've told me before you answered the door like that." It was all he could think to say because it would've changed everything.

"I'm sorry."

More deep breaths. He had to know everything now. Right now. He couldn't walk the minefield of her past without some idea of where not to step. "What else?"

"What?"

"What else do I need to know? What else haven't you told me?"

"That's it."

He nodded. Okay. He could handle this. He could handle anything for her.

"I take medication that reduces the chance that the virus will set in," she said. "But it doesn't protect you one hundred percent during sex or oral sex. So I have to ask you to wear a condom during sex and you can't go down on me and I can't give you a blowjob without protection. I can't do everything with you that I want to because he might've given me an incurable disease. I'm dirty." Her voice broke on the last word.

He glanced at her over his shoulder. It was the only movement he trusted himself to make.

She tried to cover herself with the edge of the sheet. "He made me feel dirty, and now I can't stop feeling that way. And I don't know why you want me. I'm not normal. I don't know if I can ever be normal. I'm just so tired of feeling dirty. I'm tired of being broken and dirty and ugly."

She sucked in a hiccuped breath. "And I hate the way you're looking at me right now because it makes me feel like you'll never look at me the way you used to. Always what happened to me will be all you see, and I can't take it. I can't stand that I have to make you wear a condom because being with me could kill you. And I hate that it could kill our daughter. And it's my fault."

Her words ate at him, digging at his insides until all that was left was a sharp ache for what she'd been through. So that was why she never let him go down on her. He'd figured it was a new aversion having to do with what her ex had done to her. The bastard had ruined so many things for her and here she was trying to take the blame for something that simply wasn't hers to take. "It's my fault."

"How in the hell is it your fault?" she asked, her misery punctuated with anger. "Does everything always have to revolve around you?"

"If I hadn't been so stupid and fucked around with my secretary, all of this would never have been. All of it. So yeah, I'm taking the blame because it's mine to take."

He stood across the wide, yawning gap of the bed from her, knowing nothing would ever be as it once was between them. "I swore the day you walked out of my office that I'd be better and do better. But I can't stand what happened to you. I can't stand it. It's all because of me. And I try to find a way to fix things, but then I turn around and they're so much more fucked up than I thought, and I wonder if they can ever be fixed at all.

"And then you hand me a condom and tell me that what I set in motion not only hurt you deeply, but it could kill you *and* our daughter. And I can't fucking fix that!"

"Who asked you to fix it?"

"What am I supposed to do with it?"

"Live with it just like the rest of us."

He held out a hand. "Give me the condom."

She put a knee on the bed and tentatively reached across the space to lay it in his palm. He took it between two fingers and looked at it. It wasn't like he'd never worn one. Except for those couple of times with Lucy— one of which he guessed had led to Poppy—he'd always been diligent about protection. This condom represented more than their past, it represented a potential future of medication and medical tests and suffering.

All of Cal's imaginings of more babies with Lucy dried up along with the saliva in his mouth, and he couldn't form the words that would tell her it was okay. It would be okay. Because it wasn't fucking okay, and maybe it never would be.

He set the condom on the nightstand. "Do you still want to do this?"

"Do you?"

Yes. And no. He wanted to show her that he didn't see her the way she saw herself. But he didn't think he could get it up with everything she'd said still laid out between them. She could die. Poppy could die. He'd just gotten them back, and now he could lose them.

He realized she was waiting for his answer. She was still naked, standing on the other side of the bed, watching him with that look. He hated that fucking look almost as much as he hated her ex.

"Lay down," he ordered gently.

She hesitated.

"I won. I get to choose the next five options. Lay down on the bed, darlin'."

She did as she was told, watching him with wide blue eyes. He moved to the other side of the room, grabbed the desk chair, and set it at the foot of the bed. The perfect viewing spot.

"Stay there. I'll be right back." He went into his bedroom and grabbed the things he'd need. As he came back into her room, her gaze latched on to what he held in his hand. Her intrigued look surprised him. "You like this?"

"Yes."

"Do you want it?"

"Yes."

She sounded a little hesitant and a lot curious. Good. She was going to like what he had in mind for her.

After all, it was the option she wanted to try the most.

"Fix the pillows so you're propped up higher," he told her. "That's good. Are you comfortable?"

She nodded. There was so much trust in her expression he nearly lost his nerve. He had to get this right for both of them and somehow live up to the faith she placed in him.

He set the one item on the bed next to her. Her gaze followed his movements. He leaned over her and gently placed the weighted nipple clamps on each of her nipples, adjusting the tension until she closed her eyes on a little moan.

He took his seat at the foot of the bed. Their gazes locked.

"Widen your legs," he commanded. "Wider. Now bend your knees. Drop them back so you're wide open. That's it. How're you feeling?"

"Good." Her voice was wispy now, full of expectation.

"*This,* darlin'...is option number thirty."

*

Thank you for reading FAKE! The next book in the DANGEROUS LINES series is REAL .

Cal and Lucy are closer than ever, but her ex could deny them their happily ever after.

➤CLICK HERE TO READ REAL➤

If you enjoyed FAKE, please consider leaving a review on your favorite book site. Reviews help readers find books!

➤Fake (DANGEROUS LINES novel)➤

➤GOODREADS➤

Join my VIP Facebook group Babes with Books for exclusive sneak peeks at my upcoming books & other, members only, perks:

➤www.facebook.com/groups/BabesWithBooks-ReaderGroup

Sign up to receive my newsletter for new release alerts, exclusive bonus content, and giveaways!

➤**www.bethyarnall.com/newsletter**

Turn the page to read an excerpt from REAL now!

EXCERPT FROM REAL

Option thirty.

Cal had asked her which options were her favorite on their wedding day, and Lucy had listed option thirty last even though it was the one she most wanted to try. After what she'd been forced to tell him, he'd chosen her favorite option instead of one of his own.

She lay on the bed naked, her legs wide for him. He'd placed a chair at the end of the bed, which added an extra dimension she hadn't anticipated.

"Do you trust me, darlin'?"

She nodded, her eyes wider than they'd been before.

"I'm going to sit here. I'm not allowed to move or touch you. I can't touch myself. And you're going to do everything I tell you to do, got that?"

"Yes."

"Good girl. Now we're going to start with you licking your fingers. Rub them over your nipples in small circles. "

She did as he asked, her nipples pebbling.

"Pinch them."

She took her nipples between her fingers as he'd commanded, feeling the pull deep inside. Arching her back, she pinched harder, letting out a moan.

"I love it when your cheeks flush like that. Do you like it? Do you like touching yourself?"

"Yes," she panted.

"I can tell. Are you pretending it's me, or is it just you?"

"It's me."

"You're so damn sexy, darlin'. You're making me so hard. Feel your body, how soft and voluptuous you are. Your body drives me insane. Are you wet?"

"Yes."

"How wet?"

"Not enough."

"Stroke yourself. Slide your fingers up then down. That's it."

Her breathing grew more rapid. She could see he was enjoying this, the watching. She dipped her fingers down and up, slipping into her slickness, teasing herself. Fully flush with arousal now, all she wanted to do was come.

"Arch your back a little more so the weights pull," he ordered.

She did as he asked, lifting her torso so that the weights tugged her nipples, and it was so close to how it felt when he had his hands on her that she groaned, moving her fingers faster.

"Now pick up the vibrator and switch it on."

The phallus was larger than she would've chosen for herself and had a rabbit-shaped thing at the base. She switched it on, and the ears vibrated.

"The other switch. Turn that on too."

She did, and the beads in the shaft spun while the shaft itself thrust up and down. She gasped in anticipation.

"Slide it inside you. Slowly."

She used the fingers of one hand to widen herself and inserted the vibrator as deep as it would go. She was overwhelmed with sensation. The thrusting action stroked her while the vibrating ears hit just the right spot.

"Look at me, darlin'." He was fully hard, sitting at the edge of the chair, watching her. "Do you know what I see when I look at you?" She shook her head. "I see a woman so unbelievably beautiful and sexual I want to bury myself deep inside you and pound into you until you scream my name. Do it. Move it inside you as I'd move."

She did as she was told, finding a rhythm that rocketed her toward orgasm. Opening her legs wider as the sensations built, she put her other arm above her head, pushing her breasts higher. The clamps bit down, plunging her closer to the edge.

"Faster. Harder. That's it. Fuck yourself. Come for me, darlin'. Come."

The vibration slammed into her from the front as the thrusting head hit her deep, and she went off, throwing her head back and coming so hard she cried out. Never had she felt anything so intense in her life.

The orgasm rolled through her, wave after wave of ecstasy. Nothing existed outside of her and the pulsing between her legs. She switched off the vibrator and threw it on the bed. Chest heaving and limbs tingling, she went completely limp.

"Goddammit if that wasn't the hottest thing I've ever seen."

She'd forgotten he was there. She turned her head to the side so she could look at him. "Thirty is *the best* number."

"I'm going to have it tattooed on my ass."

She laughed. "Oh, man. I needed that."

He got up from the chair, his penis hard and jutting, and lay on his stomach next to her on the bed. He kissed her shoulder right next to her scar. "You're so damn beautiful, darlin', that sometimes I can hardly breathe when I'm with you. Like right now. Your cheeks are pink and you look happy. Are you happy?"

"I think so. If happy is a loose-limbed kind of numb feeling in my arms and legs."

"That's orgasmic happiness."

She looked into his blue eyes and smiled. "Yeah. I think I am happy. More now than I used to be."

"I still have four more options, you know."

"Four." Laughing, she rolled toward him, the nipple clamps making a tinkling sound as she moved. "Are you planning on using them all tonight?"

"No. Just one more."

"Which is that?"

"This is one that I put on the list, but if you're not comfortable with it, then I'll choose another one."

"It's not one where I have to bend ways that normal people don't bend, is it?"

"Nope. It's one we've done before, so I know you can do it."

She thought of all the ways they'd had sex in the past. There were a couple she wasn't so sure if she could revisit.

"What is it?"

"Thirty-three."

"Which is that?"

"It's a really good one. In fact you can leave these on." He lifted the chain of one of the nipple clamps. "I know how much you enjoyed them."

"How does it work?"

"I lay on my back and you straddle me...backward."

The reverse cowgirl. She wasn't sure how she felt about it.

"Or you can face forward if you'd rather," he offered.

He'd chosen number thirty as the first option he'd won. He'd done it for her. The least she could do was try number thirty-three. It would give her that deep penetration she liked without having him directly behind and on top of her. She could set the pace.

"Okay," she said. "I'll try it."

*

Want to read more?

➤One-click REAL Now➤

If you loved REAL, you'll love the sexy, funny, award nominated INNOCENT serial. Cora's brother was convicted of a murder he didn't commit and it's up to her to set him free. Inspired by real cases taken on by The Innocence Project.

★ Nominated in 2017 for the Romance Writers of America Rita® award ★

➤One-click EPISODE ONE Now➤

Looking for something lighter and funny? Check out THE MISADVENTURES OF MAGGIE MAE series, starting with WAKE UP, MAGGIE, available now! Maggie has to keep her very inappropriate thoughts to herself about the FBI Special Agent assigned to protect her from a murderer.

➤One-click WAKE UP, MAGGIE Now➤

HAVE YOU BEEN ABUSED?

Your safety is important. *You're* important.
Help is available 24/7 by telephone and online.

The National Domestic Abuse Hotline

If you or someone you know is experiencing domestic violence there is help through the National Domestic Abuse hotline. Trained advocates are available to take your calls toll free, 24/7 hotline at 1-800-799-SAFE (7233).

Donations to support the hotline can be made at www.thehotline.org.

RAINN

The National Sexual Assault Online Hotline

Your privacy and safety are crucial. Please make sure you are in a safe place and that you are using a secure device and Internet connection. Please note that while we have taken numerous measures to keep your communications safe while using our site, no Internet transmission is 100% secure.

Chat online with a trained staff member who can provide you confidential crisis support.

www.rainn.org

or by phone

1-888-656-HOPE (4673)

ALSO BY BETH YARNALL

Dangerous Lines

Lost

Saved

Fake

Real

Urge

Rare

Betray

Recovered Innocence

Liberate

Exonerate

Vindicate

Innocent Serial

Episode One

Episode Two

Episode Three

The Misadventures of Maggie Mae

Wake Up, Maggie

You're Mine, Maggie

Find Me, Maggie

Azalea March Mysteries

Dyed and Gone

Beth Writing as Betty Paper

Crazy On You

Captive

Tinsel

Piano Lessons

BETH'S BOOKS FOR WRITERS

Crafting Unputdownable Fiction series

Going Deep Into Deep Point of View

Making Description Work Hard For You

Some Like It Hot: Writing Sex and Romance

ABOUT THE AUTHOR

USA Today best selling author and Rita® finalist, Beth Yarnall, writes mysteries, romantic suspense, and the occasional hilarious tweet. She lives in Southern California with her husband, two sons, and their rescue dogs where she is hard at work on her next novel. For more information about Beth and her novels please visit her website- www.bethyarnall.com

f facebook.com/bethyarnallauthor

a amazon.com/author/bethyarnall

BB bookbub.com/authors/beth-yarnall